CW01213407

BIRTHDAY BLOOD

By
Humayun

A Day of Joy Turns Deadly
Shadows of Suspicion
Secrets Behind the Smiles
Investigating the Festivities
Threads of the Past
Whispers of Envy
Playing Games with Death
The Cryptic Messages
A Midnight Visitor
Unmasking the Culprit
Motives Laid Bare
Pursuit of Justice
Lingering Shadows
Residual Fears
Closure and Reflection
The Unforgotten Mystery

A DAY OF JOY TURNS DEADLY

The quaint town of Willowbrook hummed with anticipation as preparations for the ultimate birthday bash were underway. Banners bearing the jubilant words "Happy Birthday!" fluttered in the warm summer breeze, adorning the streets and storefronts. The aroma of freshly baked goods wafted through the air, promising delightful treats to come.

Inside a charming Victorian house, the heart of the festivities was taking shape. Friends and family bustled about, carefully arranging decorations that twinkled with promise. Balloons in an array of colors adorned every corner, while streamers cascaded from the ceilings like vibrant waterfalls frozen in time. The centerpiece of it all was a grand cake, a masterpiece of fondant and frosting awaiting its moment to shine.

Amy Turner, the diligent organizer behind the event, moved with purpose as she directed the placement of each piece. With a clipboard in hand and a determined expression, she made sure no detail went overlooked. She had known the birthday boy, Daniel, for years – childhood friends turned confidantes. This celebration was meant to be a tribute to their enduring bond.

Lively chatter filled the room as guests arrived to lend a hand. Sarah, Daniel's sister, carefully hung string lights, their gentle glow promising an enchanting evening ahead. Mark, a tech-savvy friend, set up a playlist that would carry the party from sunset well into the starlit night. And then there was Mia,

Daniel's vivacious cousin, testing her culinary skills to craft an array of hors d'oeuvres that would tantalize the taste buds. Laughter and camaraderie filled the air as the group worked together. Fond memories were shared, old stories resurrected, and new jokes born on the cusp of excitement. Everyone was invested in making the celebration perfect, a reflection of Daniel's life and the happiness he had brought to theirs.

As the sun began its descent, casting a warm, golden hue over the town, the party preparations drew to a close. The finishing touches were in place, and the house glowed with the promise of revelry. Amy surveyed her creation with a mix of pride and nervousness. She hoped Daniel would love the effort they had all put into his special day.

Little did anyone know that amidst the joy and camaraderie, shadows lurked, and a sinister plot would cast a dark cloud over the celebration. The excitement that had built up would soon be shattered by a chilling event that would change their lives forever. But for now, in the golden light of dusk, the stage was set for a party that would be remembered by all who attended.

The sun's gentle rays painted the sky in shades of pink and gold as the town of Willowbrook woke up to a day of celebration. Birds chirped with an unusual enthusiasm, as if they too knew that today was no ordinary day. In the heart of the town, the Victorian house stood adorned with yesterday's care and tonight's promise, ready to embrace the day's festivities.

Inside the house, the aroma of fresh coffee mingled with the subtle scent of flowers. The party had seeped into every nook and cranny, infusing the air with an undercurrent of excitement. Upstairs in his room, Daniel awoke to the sound of a light knock on his door.

"Happy birthday, sleepyhead!" called his sister, Sarah, as she entered his room, a mischievous grin on her face. In her hands, she held a tray laden with a stack of pancakes topped with strawberries and whipped cream.

"Morning, Sarah," Daniel said with a yawn, his eyes still heavy with sleep. But as he caught sight of the feast before him, a genuine smile broke through his drowsiness. "You really outdid yourself this time."

"It's your special day, after all," she replied, placing the tray on his lap. "And you deserve the best."

The siblings chatted as Daniel savored each delicious bite, the warmth of their relationship evident in their easy camaraderie. Amidst the laughter, Sarah slipped a small envelope across the table.

"What's this?" Daniel asked, lifting an eyebrow.

"Your first birthday surprise," Sarah replied, her eyes sparkling with mischief. "Open it."

Inside the envelope, Daniel found a handwritten note that read, "A clue to unravel your day's adventure awaits you in the place where stories come to life."

He looked up at Sarah, confusion playing on his features. "What does that even mean?"

"It means you have to follow the breadcrumbs, Danny-boy," she teased. "Get ready for a scavenger hunt!"

The mention of a scavenger hunt brought a playful gleam to Daniel's eyes. Sarah had organized similar hunts in the past, and they had always led to memorable discoveries. This year was shaping up to be no different.

After breakfast, Daniel followed a series of clues that led him through the house, unlocking puzzles and riddles that made him reminisce about their shared memories. The final clue guided him to the old bookstore downtown – the place where stories truly came to life.

Stepping into the bookstore, the familiar scent of books surrounded him, wrapping him in a sense of nostalgia. At the counter, the bookstore owner handed him a beautifully wrapped package. With a grin, Daniel tore open the wrapping to reveal a leather-bound journal.

"Open it," the owner encouraged.

As Daniel flipped through the journal's pages, he found entries from family and friends, each sharing their wishes, memories, and hopes for the future. The words penned on those pages were more precious than any material gift.

The celebration had only just begun, but already, the day had been filled with love, surprises, and a deep sense of connection. As the clock ticked towards the evening, Daniel couldn't help but feel a growing anticipation for the grand party that awaited him – a party that would soon take a dark turn, shattering the very hopes that had blossomed throughout the day.

The day had transitioned from the warmth of morning to the vibrancy of midday, casting golden hues across the town of Willowbrook. The preparations for Daniel's birthday party were in full swing, the excitement tangible in the air. However, amid the laughter and joy, a creeping unease settled in the shadows.

As the clock ticked closer to the designated party hour, a delivery truck pulled up outside the Victorian house. The driver, a burly man with a perpetual scowl, handed over a package with an air of impatience. The package was large and rectangular, wrapped in dark paper that seemed to absorb the sunlight.

Inside the house, Sarah was bustling about, making sure every detail was perfect. The doorbell rang, and she hurried to answer it, surprised to find a delivery awaiting her. She signed the receipt without much thought, distracted by her many tasks, and carried the mysterious package inside.

"Daniel, there's a package for you!" she called, placing the package on the table with the rest of the decorations.

Daniel joined her, curiosity piqued. "I wasn't expecting any packages."

He gingerly unwrapped the dark paper, revealing a plain wooden box underneath. The box was intricately carved with elaborate patterns that seemed to shift and change as he examined them. It was strangely mesmerizing yet unsettling.
"What's inside?" Sarah asked, her eyes curious.
Daniel hesitated, a sense of foreboding tugging at the edges of his consciousness. He slowly opened the box, revealing a single item: a miniature hourglass. The sands within trickled down with an almost hypnotic rhythm.
"It's… interesting," Daniel said, his brow furrowing. "But who sent it? And why?"
As if on cue, a slip of paper fluttered out from the box and landed on the table. Sarah picked it up and read aloud, "Tick-tock, Daniel, the sands of time are running out. The past haunts the present, and your celebration will reveal what's hidden."
The room fell into a heavy silence, the weight of the message sinking in. It was as if the jovial atmosphere had been punctured, replaced by an eerie undercurrent of tension. The message seemed cryptic, a puzzle with missing pieces.
"This isn't some elaborate prank, is it?" Sarah asked, her concern evident.
Daniel shook his head. "I don't know. It doesn't feel like one. But whoever sent this – they know something."
The party that was meant to be a joyful celebration had taken an unexpected turn. The enigmatic gift had cast a shadow over the day's events, leaving a trail of questions in its wake. The once-clear narrative of Daniel's birthday had morphed into something darker, something that would lead them down a rabbit hole of mystery and intrigue. As the hourglass continued to trickle its sands, the countdown to the truth had begun, and the party was about to take a chilling twist.

SHADOWS OF SUSPICION

As the afternoon sun cast long shadows across the streets of Willowbrook, the atmosphere in the Victorian house was one of anticipation and growing concern. The unsettling gift had cast a shadow over Daniel's birthday celebrations, leaving everyone on edge. The party was set to begin soon, yet there was an unspoken tension that hung in the air.

Guests arrived one by one, their cheerful greetings masking the unease that had settled among them. Amy, who had been at the heart of the party planning, exchanged worried glances with Sarah as the minutes ticked away. Daniel mingled with the guests, trying his best to maintain a facade of normalcy, though his thoughts kept drifting back to the enigmatic message and the ominous hourglass.

As the designated start time for the party came and went, it became increasingly clear that someone vital was missing: Evan, Daniel's closest childhood friend. Evan was known for his punctuality and had never missed a birthday celebration. His absence was unsettling, given the mysterious circumstances that had already begun to unfold.

Amy discreetly approached Sarah, her expression concerned. "Have you heard from Evan at all?"

Sarah shook her head, her brow furrowed. "No, and it's not like him to just vanish without a word."

Amy's gaze shifted to the corner of the room, where a small group of friends huddled together, their voices hushed. Mark, who was known for his tech savvy, seemed to be showing something on his phone to the others.

"What's going on?" Sarah asked, her curiosity piqued.

Mark approached them, his expression a mix of worry and intrigue. "Take a look at this."

He showed them a social media post that had been shared by Evan's account. The post depicted a cryptic image of an hourglass – the same hourglass from the sinister gift – along with a caption that read, "Time waits for no one."

"That's definitely strange," Daniel commented, his gaze fixed on the post. "Evan wasn't acting like this earlier."

Sarah's eyes narrowed as she analyzed the post. "This feels like more than just a prank."

"Agreed," Amy chimed in. "We should try to reach out to him, make sure he's okay."

They attempted to call Evan, but each call went unanswered, leaving a growing sense of unease in its wake. As the minutes turned into hours, the party's atmosphere became increasingly somber. Laughter was replaced by hushed conversations and worried glances exchanged between guests.

The clock struck the hour, and Amy approached Daniel, her voice soft with concern. "Maybe we should postpone the party. It doesn't feel right to celebrate with Evan missing."

Daniel nodded in agreement. "You're right. Let's make an announcement."

The atmosphere that had once been filled with excitement and joy was now tinged with worry and uncertainty. The party, which had promised to be a celebration of life and friendship, had been derailed by the shadows of an enigma that had taken hold of the day. As the group gathered, their voices united in a chorus of concern, they couldn't shake the feeling that something ominous was unfolding, something that went beyond a simple birthday celebration.

As the sun dipped below the horizon, casting a warm glow over the town of Willowbrook, the atmosphere inside the Victorian house had taken a sharp turn. What was supposed to be a joyous celebration had transformed into a search for answers, with Evan's mysterious disappearance casting a dark shadow over the evening.

Guests exchanged worried glances and hushed conversations, their initial excitement now replaced with a sense of urgency. Daniel, surrounded by his closest friends and family, felt a growing unease gnawing at him. The message, the hourglass, and now Evan's absence – they were all connected somehow, but how, and why?

With a heavy sigh, Daniel excused himself from a group of friends and approached Amy, who was deep in conversation with Sarah and Mark. He cleared his throat, capturing their attention.

"I don't know about you all, but I can't shake this feeling that something's seriously wrong," Daniel admitted, his voice laced with worry.

Sarah nodded in agreement. "It's like we're missing a piece of the puzzle, and until we find out what's going on with Evan, we won't be able to piece it all together."

Amy glanced around the room, her gaze settling on the clock that ticked steadily on the wall. "We should definitely keep trying to reach him. And maybe even involve the authorities if necessary."

As if on cue, Mark's phone buzzed with an incoming call. He picked it up and furrowed his brow, his expression growing more serious. "It's Evan's number," he said, answering the call. The room fell into a tense silence as Mark listened to the voice on the other end. His face paled, and he nodded occasionally as if responding to something being said. After what felt like an eternity, he hung up the call and turned to face the group.

"That was Evan's roommate," Mark began, his voice heavy. "He said Evan left home earlier today, claiming he had some important errands to run. But he hasn't been answering his calls or texts since then."

Amy folded her arms, her expression a mix of worry and frustration. "This doesn't make any sense. Why would he just disappear like this?"

"Maybe he found something related to that message and the hourglass," Daniel suggested, his mind racing with possibilities.

Mark nodded in agreement. "It's a possibility. Whatever it is, it seems like Evan stumbled upon something that has him spooked."

Sarah sighed, her concern evident. "We need to find him and make sure he's safe."

With a determined nod, Daniel looked around at his friends and family. "Let's split up and start searching. We can cover more ground that way."

As the group mobilized, making calls, sending messages, and coordinating search efforts, the once-bustling house emptied out. The laughter and excitement of the party had given way to a shared determination to uncover the truth behind Evan's disappearance and the sinister events that had unfolded throughout the day.

The night air was cool, and the stars began to twinkle in the sky as they dispersed, each driven by a singular goal: to find Evan, to piece together the puzzle, and to bring an end to the enigma that had gripped their celebration.

Under the cover of the night sky, the town of Willowbrook was a hive of activity. Friends and family fanned out across the streets, peering into shadows and calling out Evan's name. Each step felt heavier as the reality of the situation sank in – a beloved friend was missing, and they were determined to unravel the mystery that had taken hold of their celebration.

Back at the Victorian house, the atmosphere remained tense as those who had not joined the search huddled together, their thoughts swirling with theories and unanswered questions.

Amy, Sarah, Mark, and Daniel had reconvened in the living room, each with a notepad in hand and a determined look on their faces.

"We need to gather everything we know so far and see if we can make sense of it," Amy suggested, her voice a mix of determination and worry.

Mark nodded, tapping his pen against his notepad. "Agreed. Let's start with the message and the hourglass. They're the most concrete clues we have."

Daniel leaned forward, his brow furrowed. "The message mentioned the past haunting the present. What could that mean?"

Sarah chimed in, her expression thoughtful. "Maybe it's about something that happened in the past – a secret, a grudge – something that's resurfacing now."

Amy crossed her arms, her gaze fixed on the floor as if lost in thought. "And the hourglass might symbolize time running out, urgency. But what's running out? Evan's time? Ours?"

Mark tapped his pen on his notepad. "Let's not forget the image Evan posted – the hourglass. Maybe it's pointing us to something – a location, an object?"

As they discussed and debated, the pieces of the puzzle slowly began to fit together, though the full picture remained elusive. Each theory led to another question, every potential answer branching into new avenues of investigation.

"What if the clues are connected to the party itself?" Sarah mused, her eyes lighting up. "The hourglass gift, the message – maybe it's something we're supposed to find here?"

Daniel's gaze shifted to the corner of the room where the gift had been placed, untouched since its arrival. With a determined nod, he stood up. "Let's take a closer look at that hourglass. Maybe there's something we missed."

They gathered around the wooden box, their eyes fixed on the intricate carvings. Daniel carefully picked up the hourglass, examining it from every angle. Sarah pulled out her phone and snapped a photo, zooming in on the patterns etched into the wood.

"Wait a minute," Mark said, leaning closer. "Do you see those markings? They look like coordinates."

Amy squinted, her excitement growing. "Coordinates? As in, geographic coordinates?"

Mark nodded, his fingers dancing across his phone's screen. "Exactly. If we plug these coordinates into a map app, we might find something."

Within moments, Mark had the coordinates entered, and a map appeared on the screen, showing a location just outside of town.

"That's not far from here," Daniel said, his voice a mix of hope and urgency. "Let's go check it out."

As they prepared to head out into the night, the group's determination was palpable. The theories and conjectures had led them to a potential breakthrough, a thread of hope in the midst of uncertainty. With Evan's disappearance and the ominous events of the day driving them forward, they set out on a new path, ready to uncover the truth that lay hidden in the shadows of their celebration.

SECRETS BEHIND THE SMILES

The night air was cool and crisp as Daniel, Sarah, Amy, and Mark ventured outside the Victorian house, their steps guided by the coordinates discovered on the enigmatic hourglass. The town of Willowbrook seemed different under the cover of darkness – quieter, more mysterious, and full of potential secrets waiting to be unraveled.

The coordinates led them to an old abandoned factory at the outskirts of town. The building stood like a sentinel of the past, its windows shattered and walls worn by time. Moonlight cast eerie shadows as the group approached cautiously, their footsteps echoing in the silence.

"Are we sure this is the right place?" Sarah whispered, her gaze fixed on the dilapidated structure.

Mark nodded, holding up his phone with the map displayed. "According to the coordinates, this is the spot."

Daniel took a deep breath, his heart racing. "Alright, let's see if we can find anything that might lead us to Evan."

They ventured inside the factory, their footsteps echoing in the cavernous space. The beams of their flashlights cut through the darkness, revealing a landscape of rusted machinery and discarded debris. As they explored further, a sense of unease settled over them – the factory seemed to hold secrets of its own, waiting to be uncovered.

After what felt like an eternity, Amy's voice broke the silence. "Look over there."

They directed their lights to where Amy was pointing, revealing a door that seemed oddly out of place amidst the decay. Daniel approached the door cautiously, his heart pounding. With a deep breath, he pushed it open, revealing a small room beyond.

Inside, they found a collection of old files, photographs, and newspaper clippings strewn across a dusty table. It was as if they had stumbled upon a hidden archive of the town's history.

Mark began sifting through the documents, his eyes widening as he made a discovery. "These are news articles from years ago – unsolved mysteries, disappearances, strange occurrences."

Amy picked up a faded photograph, her expression pensive. "And look at this – it's a picture of Evan's family."

Sarah's eyes narrowed. "What would Evan's family be doing here, hidden away in this place?"

As they delved deeper into the files, a pattern emerged – the factory was connected to a series of unsolved incidents that had haunted Willowbrook for years. Disappearances, strange phenomena, all linked to this seemingly innocuous location.

"Could Evan have uncovered something about his own family's past?" Daniel wondered aloud, his mind racing.

Mark looked up from the documents, his voice tense. "Or could Evan's family be connected to these incidents?"

The implications were chilling. The facade of normalcy that Willowbrook had presented was unraveling, revealing hidden tensions and secrets that had been buried for decades. The celebration that was meant to bring people together had inadvertently torn away the veneer, exposing a tangled web of mysteries and unanswered questions.

As they left the factory, the weight of their discoveries hung heavily in the air. The town had taken on a new aura – one of uncertainty and intrigue. With each step, the group felt a renewed determination to find Evan and unravel the enigma that had consumed their celebration. The truth was out there, waiting to be unveiled, no matter how dark or unsettling it might be.

The moon hung low in the sky as Daniel, Sarah, Amy, and Mark reconvened at the Victorian house after their unsettling discovery at the abandoned factory. The weight of the night's revelations lingered in the air, leaving a sense of unease that had settled deep within them. The town of Willowbrook, once a quaint and peaceful place, now felt like a labyrinth of hidden tensions and long-forgotten grudges.

Gathered around the living room, the group sifted through the documents and photographs they had found. The images painted a picture of a town with a history fraught with unresolved mysteries and disappearances – incidents that had been buried beneath the surface for years.

"Could Evan's family be somehow tied to all of this?" Sarah mused, her voice tinged with concern.

Amy nodded, her brow furrowed. "It seems likely. But we need more information to connect the dots."

Mark tapped a finger against the table, his expression thoughtful. "We know Evan's family has a connection to this place, and the hourglass led us here. But what's the link between the past and the present?"

Daniel leaned back in his chair, his gaze fixed on the old photographs. "Maybe it's not just Evan's family. Maybe there are other families with ties to this place."

As they examined the photos, names began to resurface – names of families that had lived in Willowbrook for generations, names that seemed to be connected by a thread of secrecy and unease.

"I remember hearing stories about old feuds and rivalries in this town," Sarah said, her voice pensive. "Could those be tied to the disappearances?"

Amy nodded, her eyes narrowing as she recalled the whispers she had heard from the townspeople. "There's a history of grudges and conflicts that go back years. It's like a web of relationships that no one wants to talk about."

Mark's eyes lit up as a thought crossed his mind. "What if Evan stumbled upon some sort of journal or account of these past events? Maybe that's what he found here."

Their theories were beginning to converge, forming a clearer picture of the connection between the past and the present. Evan's disappearance, the ominous message, the hourglass, and the tangled history of Willowbrook all seemed to intersect at a nexus of secrets waiting to be unraveled.

"We need to keep digging," Daniel said, his voice firm. "We need to find Evan and get to the bottom of this."

With renewed determination, the group made a plan to continue their investigation. They would reach out to anyone who had lived in Willowbrook for generations, anyone who might have stories or insights into the history that had been obscured by time and silence.

As the night wore on, the moonlight casting a pale glow through the windows, they realized that the journey they had embarked upon was not just about solving a mystery – it was about uncovering the truth behind the facade, about unearthing the hidden tensions and rivalries that had festered beneath the surface for far too long. The web of relationships that had ensnared the town was unraveling, and they were determined to see it through to the end, no matter how unsettling the truth might be.

The sun rose on a new day in Willowbrook, casting a soft, golden light that belied the turmoil that had consumed the town. The events of the past few days had left a palpable sense of unease, and the group's investigation into Evan's disappearance and the town's hidden history had uncovered layers of secrets that had long been buried.

Daniel, Sarah, Amy, and Mark had spent the night poring over old records, photographs, and even speaking to some of the town's older residents. The stories they had heard were unsettling – tales of feuds, betrayals, and rivalries that had festered behind closed doors for generations.

Sitting around the table in the Victorian house, their faces drawn with exhaustion, they shared what they had learned. The web of relationships that had once seemed innocuous was now a complex tapestry of deceit and hidden agendas.

"Everyone seemed to have a secret, something they didn't want to talk about," Amy said, her voice tinged with frustration.

Mark nodded, his expression troubled. "It's like the whole town has been living with this weight of the past on their shoulders."

Sarah leaned forward, her gaze fixed on the old photographs strewn across the table. "And we know that Evan's family was somehow connected to this history. But how?"

Daniel tapped his fingers against the table, lost in thought. "Maybe it's not just about one family. Maybe it's about all of them – about the town's collective history."

Amy sighed, running a hand through her hair. "We need to find Evan and get his perspective on all of this. He might have found something that could tie everything together."

As if on cue, Mark's phone buzzed with a new message. He picked it up, his eyes widening as he read the text. "It's from Evan. He's asking to meet us tonight."

The news brought a mixture of relief and anticipation. With newfound determination, they spent the day organizing their findings, putting together a timeline of events, and preparing questions for Evan.

The sun dipped below the horizon, and the group gathered once again in the living room, their excitement palpable. The anticipation was tempered by the realization that the revelations that awaited them might shatter their perceptions of the town they had known.

Evan arrived, his expression a mix of weariness and determination. As he recounted his own discoveries and the events that had led him to the abandoned factory, the pieces of the puzzle began to fit together. Evan's family had been intertwined with the town's history, and the truth he had uncovered was far more sinister than anyone could have imagined.

"The stories we've heard, the rivalries, the secrets – they all lead to this," Evan said, his voice heavy with emotion. "It's about power, control, and a web of deceit that's been spun for generations."

The truth was a tapestry of betrayal and hidden agendas, one that had been carefully woven over the years to protect the reputation of those involved. The celebration that had been meant to bring joy had instead unraveled a history of darkness that had cast a shadow over the town for far too long.

As the night wore on, the group grappled with the weight of their discoveries. The facade that had once shielded the town's secrets had been torn apart, and they were left to face a reality that was both unsettling and heartbreaking. With the truth finally revealed, they were determined to bring justice to the past and shed light on the darkness that had plagued Willowbrook for generations.

INVESTIGATING THE FESTIVITIES

The moon hung high in the night sky, casting a silvery glow over the town of Willowbrook. The revelations of the past few days had left the town reeling, and the sense of unease was almost palpable. The group had unearthed the truth behind Evan's disappearance and the town's hidden history, but their discoveries had opened a Pandora's box of darkness and deceit.
As the night wore on, a new figure arrived in Willowbrook – Detective Maria Thompson. Known for her keen investigative skills, she was renowned for solving some of the most complex cases in the region. Her presence brought a sense of authority and focus to the situation, as she joined the group in the living room of the Victorian house.
"I've reviewed the information you provided and the evidence you've collected," Detective Thompson said, her tone measured. "It's clear that there's a lot more to this than meets the eye."
The group nodded, their expressions a mix of anticipation and apprehension. They had gathered photographs, documents, and their own accounts of the events that had unfolded, hoping that Detective Thompson could help them piece together the final parts of the puzzle.
"Let's start from the beginning," she said, her gaze fixed on the files spread across the table. "We know that Evan's disappearance is tied to the history of this town, and that

there's a connection to various families. But what's the motive behind it all?"

As they recounted their findings, Detective Thompson listened intently, occasionally asking probing questions that revealed a depth of insight into the workings of criminal investigations. She examined the photographs, newspaper clippings, and other evidence they had collected, her mind working to form connections and patterns.

"It's clear that the rivalry and animosities between these families have been festering for a long time," she mused. "And Evan's discovery of this hidden history must have triggered something."

Mark leaned forward, his voice earnest. "Do you think there's a possibility that someone wanted to silence Evan because of what he uncovered?"

Detective Thompson nodded, her eyes thoughtful. "It's a valid theory. Whoever is behind this may have seen Evan as a threat to their secrets."

Amy sighed, her expression a mix of frustration and determination. "But how do we prove any of this? How do we find the evidence we need to bring those responsible to justice?"

The detective's gaze met theirs, her expression resolute. "We start by examining the crime scene where you found the documents. There might be something there – a clue, a piece of evidence – that could lead us to the person responsible."

With renewed purpose, the group prepared to revisit the abandoned factory. The night air was cold and still as they entered the building, flashlights in hand, accompanied by Detective Thompson. They combed through the room, scrutinizing every inch, hoping to find the missing link that would reveal the identity of Evan's assailant.

As they explored further, Mark's voice broke the silence. "Over here – look at this."

The group gathered around him, their flashlights revealing a hidden compartment in the wall. Inside, they found a bundle of letters, photographs, and documents that seemed to be connected to the events they had uncovered.

Detective Thompson's eyes narrowed as she examined the contents. "These seem to be personal correspondences, a trail of information that someone didn't want others to find."

As they pieced together the puzzle, it became clear that the factory had been used as a repository for the town's darkest secrets. The documents contained references to betrayals, cover-ups, and even threats – evidence that someone was willing to go to great lengths to protect their interests.

With newfound determination, they left the factory, their minds racing with the implications of their discovery. The detective's arrival had brought a fresh perspective to the investigation, and the evidence they had found was a promising step towards unmasking the person behind the web of deception that had ensnared Willowbrook for generations.

As the night pressed on, the group knew that their journey was far from over. With each new revelation, each uncovered clue, they were one step closer to unraveling the truth and bringing justice to a town haunted by its past.

The morning sun bathed Willowbrook in soft light, casting a sense of calm over the town. Inside the Victorian house, however, the atmosphere was charged with purpose. The group had made significant progress in their investigation, uncovering evidence that pointed to a web of secrets and deceit. Now, armed with Detective Maria Thompson's guidance, they turned their attention to the people who had been present at Daniel's ill-fated birthday party.

The living room had been transformed into a makeshift interview room, complete with notebooks, pens, and recording equipment. Detective Thompson, with her seasoned experience, directed the proceedings.

"We need to establish alibis and gather testimonies from everyone who attended the party," she explained. "We'll piece together a timeline of events leading up to Evan's disappearance."

One by one, partygoers were brought in for questioning. Each interview was conducted with care, as the group sought to uncover any clues or discrepancies that might shed light on the truth. As the interviews progressed, patterns began to emerge.

"Tell me about your interactions with Evan at the party," Detective Thompson asked one of the guests.

The woman fidgeted slightly, her gaze shifting. "I saw him a couple of times. He seemed a bit distracted."

"Did he mention anything specific?" Detective Thompson pressed.

"He did mention something about looking into the history of the town," she replied hesitantly.

The interviews continued, with each person offering their own perspective on the party and the hours leading up to Evan's disappearance. Some remembered Evan being preoccupied, others recalled him engaged in animated conversations. The detective's questions probed for any inconsistencies or unusual behaviors.

As the interviews progressed, a clearer timeline began to take shape. The group compiled the information, noting down potential points of interest and individuals who warranted further investigation.

"Are there any commonalities among the testimonies?" Amy mused, reviewing her notes.

Sarah nodded, her expression thoughtful. "Several people mentioned seeing Evan near the end of the party, around the time when things were winding down."

Daniel leaned back in his chair, deep in thought. "That could be a crucial point. If Evan was acting differently towards the end, it might provide a clue about what happened next."

Mark added, "We also need to cross-reference these accounts with the evidence we found at the factory. There might be connections that we're missing."

Detective Thompson joined them, her demeanor focused. "I'll take the evidence we've collected and see if any of it matches the testimonies we've gathered. We're looking for inconsistencies, overlaps, anything that could guide us."

As the group reviewed their findings, the weight of their investigation settled upon them. The truth was elusive, but each interview, each piece of evidence, brought them closer to unraveling the mystery that had enveloped their town.

With renewed determination, they pressed forward, knowing that the answers lay within the web of relationships, rivalries, and secrets that had plagued Willowbrook for generations. The alibis and testimonies of the partygoers were puzzle pieces waiting to be fitted together, and with each piece, the truth drew nearer.

As the sun set once again over Willowbrook, the group's determination burned brighter than ever. With partygoer interviews and evidence collection underway, they focused on a critical aspect of their investigation – the hours leading up to Evan's disappearance. The detective and her team worked tirelessly to recreate the timeline of the evening, hoping to uncover the truth hidden within the gaps.

The living room had been transformed into a makeshift war room, filled with maps, photographs, and a detailed schedule of events. The group gathered around the table, the atmosphere charged with a mixture of anticipation and tension.

"We know that Evan was seen near the end of the party," Detective Thompson began, her gaze fixed on the timeline they had created. "But what happened in those missing hours leading up to that point?"

Mark tapped his pen against the table, lost in thought. "We need to account for everyone's movements during that time.

Who interacted with Evan, what conversations took place – anything that could provide a lead."

As they discussed their plan of action, each member of the group took on a specific task. They reviewed the interviews, cross-referenced testimonies with evidence, and began to piece together a clearer picture of what had transpired.

Sarah pointed to the timeline, her voice determined. "We know that Evan was particularly interested in the history of the town. Perhaps he shared his findings with someone, and that triggered a reaction."

Amy nodded in agreement. "If someone perceived Evan's discoveries as a threat, they might have confronted him during those missing hours."

Daniel leaned over the table, his expression resolute. "We need to identify the key players during that time. Who were the individuals who interacted with Evan, and what were the nature of their conversations?"

As they delved deeper into the timeline, connections began to emerge. Conversations, confrontations, and even small gestures took on new significance as the pieces of the puzzle started to fit together. The detective's keen insights guided their analysis, as they focused on the most crucial moments of the evening.

"Look at this," Mark said, his finger tracing a path on the timeline. "Evan had a lengthy conversation with one of the town's oldest residents, Mr. Hawthorne."

Detective Thompson's eyes narrowed. "And what was the nature of their conversation?"

Amy reviewed her notes. "According to Mr. Hawthorne's testimony, Evan was asking about the factory and the town's history. Mr. Hawthorne seemed defensive, dismissive even."

The detective's gaze met theirs, her expression thoughtful. "That could be a point of interest. Let's dig deeper into Mr. Hawthorne's connection to the factory and the town's history."

With a renewed focus, they began to unravel Mr. Hawthorne's role in the events leading up to Evan's disappearance. As they pieced together the puzzle, the missing hours of that evening began to come into sharper focus, revealing a narrative that was both intriguing and unsettling.

The room was filled with the sound of rustling papers, hushed conversations, and the clicking of pens against notepads. Each discovery, each revelation, was a step closer to uncovering the truth that had remained hidden for far too long.

As the night grew darker, the group's determination burned like a beacon in the midst of uncertainty. The missing hours were no longer a void, but a canvas on which they were painstakingly painting the story of the town's secrets and Evan's fateful evening. With each piece of the puzzle they uncovered, they were closer to unmasking the truth and bringing justice to a town haunted by its past.

THREADS OF THE PAST

The sun rose over Willowbrook, casting a warm glow over the town. The investigation into Evan's disappearance had brought to light a complex web of secrets and hidden tensions that had festered for generations. The group had made significant progress, piecing together the events of the fateful evening and the town's history, but there were still missing links that needed to be uncovered.

As they gathered once again in the living room of the Victorian house, a new idea began to take shape. Daniel's childhood held key insights into the town's past, and the relationships he had formed might hold clues to the mystery they were unraveling.

"Let's focus on Daniel's early years," Detective Thompson suggested. "Childhood friendships and rivalries often provide valuable insights into the dynamics of a community."

Daniel's eyes lit up as he considered the possibilities. "I grew up here, spent my whole childhood in Willowbrook. I have connections that go back a long way."

Amy leaned forward, her expression thoughtful. "Your friendships and experiences might shed light on the motivations of the people involved. Childhood grievances and alliances could be significant."

Mark nodded in agreement. "And if Evan stumbled upon something related to the past, it might have resonated with your memories."

With renewed determination, they began to delve into Daniel's childhood connections. They reviewed old yearbooks, photographs, and even spoke to some of Daniel's childhood friends who still lived in the town. Each conversation revealed a piece of the puzzle, offering glimpses into the past that had shaped the present.

One friend, Jake, shared stories of their adventures as kids, exploring the woods and playing in abandoned places. He mentioned that Daniel and Evan had often been inseparable during their early years, sharing a fascination with mysteries and hidden places.

"Wait, I remember something," Daniel said, his voice tinged with excitement. "There was a story we used to talk about – a legend in Willowbrook about a hidden treasure. We'd explore old buildings, trying to find clues."

Detective Thompson leaned forward, intrigued. "A hidden treasure? That could be significant. It might have some connection to the factory or the town's history."

Amy chimed in, her eyes bright. "If Evan had been researching the town's history, he might have stumbled upon that same legend."

As they explored the possibility of a hidden treasure, they began to piece together a new theory – that Evan's disappearance might be connected to his pursuit of the town's secrets, including the fabled treasure that had captured the imagination of children for generations.

Sarah reviewed the timeline they had constructed, her voice thoughtful. "If Evan's investigations led him to uncover something tied to the past – something that some people wanted to keep hidden – it could explain why he vanished."

With each connection they made, each revelation they uncovered, the puzzle grew clearer. The town's history, Daniel's childhood friendships, and Evan's pursuits were all threads woven together in a complex narrative. The group knew that they were on the brink of discovering the truth that had been concealed for far too long.

As the day progressed, their determination remained unshakeable. They were piecing together a story that spanned generations, uncovering the motivations, rivalries, and alliances that had shaped Willowbrook's past and present. The mysteries that had haunted the town for years were finally being brought to light, and with each new revelation, they were one step closer to solving the enigma that had gripped them all.

The days in Willowbrook seemed to stretch on as the investigation into Evan's disappearance continued. With every new piece of information they uncovered, the town's history grew more intricate, revealing a tapestry of forgotten wounds and old heartaches. As the group delved deeper, they realized that the events of the present were intricately tied to the grievances of the past.

Sitting around the table in the Victorian house, the group reviewed the latest findings, tracing connections between Daniel's childhood friendships, Evan's investigations, and the town's history.

"It's clear that the legend of the hidden treasure is more than just a childhood story," Detective Thompson said, her voice tinged with conviction. "It holds a key to understanding the motivations behind Evan's disappearance."

Mark nodded, his gaze fixed on the maps and documents spread out before them. "And if Evan had uncovered something related to that legend, it might have resurfaced old wounds and rivalries."

Sarah leaned forward, her expression pensive. "We've heard stories of feuds and betrayals that go back generations. Could this treasure be tied to those conflicts?"

Daniel's voice was heavy with realization. "Maybe the treasure isn't just a physical object. Maybe it symbolizes something that people are willing to fight for – power, control, pride."

As they explored the connection between the hidden treasure, the town's history, and Evan's investigations, they began to unravel a complex web of motivations. Grudges that had been buried for years were resurfacing, and the wounds of the past were bleeding into the present.

Amy reviewed her notes, her voice measured. "We need to speak to more people who have knowledge of the town's history. They might be able to provide insights into how these old hurts and heartaches are connected to the present."

The group set out to interview older residents who had lived in Willowbrook for decades, hoping to gather stories and perspectives that could shed light on the town's complicated dynamics. As they listened to tales of lost opportunities, broken friendships, and simmering animosities, the pieces of the puzzle fell into place.

One woman, Mrs. Thompson, shared a story from her childhood about a dispute between two families over land rights. She mentioned that the dispute had never been fully resolved and had led to a rift that persisted through the generations.

Detective Thompson's eyes lit up as she made a connection. "Could this unresolved dispute be linked to the treasure? If the treasure holds some sort of significance, it could be a symbol of victory or redemption."

Sarah nodded, her voice determined. "And if Evan had been on the brink of uncovering this truth, it could explain why someone might have wanted to silence him."

The group's collective understanding deepened as the threads of the past and present wove together into a narrative of hurt and longing. The investigation was no longer just about solving a mystery – it was about uncovering the stories that had shaped the town, unearthing the forgotten wounds that had festered over the years, and seeking justice for a disappearance that was rooted in a complex tapestry of emotions and motivations.

With each interview, each revelation, they were drawing closer to the heart of the matter. The town's history was becoming more tangible, its pain and conflict more real. And as they continued to explore the connections between the hidden treasure, the rivalries, and the present events, they knew that the truth they were seeking was within reach, waiting to be uncovered and understood.

The town of Willowbrook seemed to hold its breath as the investigation into Evan's disappearance continued. The group had unraveled a complex web of connections between childhood friendships, forgotten grudges, and the pursuit of a hidden treasure. With each new piece of information, they felt that they were drawing closer to understanding the motives behind Evan's vanishing.

The living room of the Victorian house had become a hub of activity, filled with maps, notes, and photographs that chronicled the town's history. The group's determination burned brighter than ever as they worked to decipher the motivations that had led to the fateful events of Daniel's birthday.

Daniel reviewed the old photographs, his gaze fixed on a group of children that included Evan and himself. "We were just kids, exploring the woods and imagining hidden treasures. Who would've thought it would lead to all of this?"

Detective Thompson leaned against the table, her expression thoughtful. "Sometimes, childhood dreams and adventures hold more significance than we realize. They can become the seeds from which bigger stories grow."

Mark pointed to a map, tracing a line that connected the abandoned factory to various locations in town. "The factory seems to be at the center of everything – the town's history, Evan's investigation, the hidden treasure. It's like a focal point."

Amy nodded, her voice determined. "If we can uncover the significance of the factory, we might understand why it became the epicenter of these events."

As they delved into the history of the factory, they discovered that it had once been a thriving hub of industry, a place where families had worked for generations. But as the years passed, the factory fell into disrepair, and the memories of its past began to fade.

Sarah glanced at an old newspaper clipping, her voice thoughtful. "According to this article, there was a dispute over the factory's ownership decades ago. Two families, the Montgomerys and the Harrisons, fought over it."

Detective Thompson's eyes lit up with recognition. "The Montgomerys and the Harrisons – those are names that have come up repeatedly in our investigation."

The connections were becoming clearer – the dispute over the factory's ownership, the town's history of rivalries, and the hidden treasure that had captured the imaginations of children like Evan and Daniel. The past was interwoven with the present in ways they had never anticipated.

Daniel's voice was tinged with realization. "If Evan had stumbled upon evidence of the factory's history – evidence that might have resolved the dispute or uncovered the treasure – someone might have seen him as a threat."

Amy's gaze met his, her expression determined. "And that someone might have been connected to the Montgomerys or the Harrisons, someone who was willing to go to great lengths to protect their family's interests."

The room was filled with a mix of excitement and apprehension as the pieces of the puzzle fell into place. The hidden motives, the buried grievances, and the pursuit of the truth were all coming together in a narrative that was both intricate and compelling.

With newfound clarity, the group knew that they were on the brink of a breakthrough. The history of the factory, the rivalry between the families, and the motivations behind Evan's disappearance were intertwined in a way that painted a vivid picture of the events that had unfolded. As they continued to search for clues within the town's history, they were confident that the truth was finally within their grasp, waiting to be uncovered and brought into the light.

WHISPERS OF ENVY

The sun cast long shadows as it dipped below the horizon, signaling the approach of another night in Willowbrook. The investigation into Evan's disappearance had taken the group on a journey through the town's history, unearthing rivalries, hidden motives, and a web of secrets. With each step, they had grown closer to the truth, and the pieces of the puzzle were finally falling into place.

The living room of the Victorian house was bathed in a soft, golden light as the group gathered to review their progress. The map of the town's history, covered in notes and threads, served as a visual representation of the connections they had made.

Daniel's voice was filled with determination as he looked at the map. "The factory, the hidden treasure, the rivalry between the Montgomerys and the Harrisons – they're all connected. Evan's investigation must have triggered something that someone wanted to keep hidden."

Detective Thompson nodded, her gaze fixed on the map. "Our focus now is to identify who within these families might have had a motive to silence Evan."

Mark leaned over the table, his expression thoughtful. "Jealousy and resentment could play a significant role. If Evan was close to uncovering something that threatened someone's status or reputation, it could have led to desperate actions."

Amy reviewed her notes, her voice steady. "We've heard stories of family disputes, lost opportunities, and old wounds.

Those emotions can fester over time and drive people to do things they might not have otherwise considered."

Sarah's eyes narrowed as she studied the map. "We need to pinpoint individuals who might have felt threatened by Evan's investigations, individuals who had a lot to lose if the truth came out."

The detective began to piece together a list of potential suspects – individuals who had ties to the Montgomerys and the Harrisons, individuals who might have been fueled by jealousy or resentment.

"Let's start by examining the movements and actions of these individuals around the time of the party," Detective Thompson suggested. "We'll look for any patterns or behaviors that might stand out."

As they delved into the suspects' backgrounds, they discovered a trail of information that hinted at hidden motives and suppressed emotions. There were accounts of failed business ventures, lost opportunities, and simmering rivalries that had never been fully resolved.

"We need to speak to these individuals," Daniel said, his voice firm. "We need to confront them with what we know and see how they react."

The group agreed, and a plan was set into motion. They would approach the suspects one by one, presenting their findings and gauging their reactions. The hope was that someone's behavior, a slip of the tongue, or a telltale sign of guilt might reveal the truth they had been seeking.

The sun had set completely, leaving the room bathed in the soft glow of lamplight as the group finalized their strategy. The town's history, the web of relationships, and the emotions that had driven Evan's disappearance were all converging in a narrative that was both intricate and captivating.

With a sense of purpose, they knew that they were about to confront the green-eyed suspects who might hold the answers to the questions that had haunted them for days. As they prepared to uncover the truth, they were resolved to see the investigation through to its conclusion, no matter how unsettling the revelations might be.

The moon hung high in the sky, casting a silvery glow over Willowbrook. Inside the Victorian house, the atmosphere was charged with anticipation and resolve. The group had identified potential suspects within the Montgomery and Harrison families, individuals who might have been driven by jealousy and resentment to silence Evan and protect their secrets.

As they gathered in the living room, Detective Thompson reviewed the profiles of the suspects they had compiled. "These individuals have ties to the town's history, and there are indications that they might have had motives to prevent Evan from uncovering the truth."

Daniel leaned forward, his expression determined. "We need to speak to each of them, confront them with what we know, and see if we can get any reactions that might reveal their guilt."

Amy nodded, her eyes focused. "We'll be looking for signs of discomfort, inconsistencies in their stories, anything that might give us a clue about their involvement."

Sarah added, "If Evan was close to revealing something that threatened their positions or reputations, it's possible that we might see their true colors emerge."

With their strategy in place, they set out to interview the suspects. The first on the list was Emily Montgomery, a member of the Montgomery family who had a history of conflicts with Evan's family. The group arranged to meet her at a local café, where they could discuss their findings discreetly.

Emily's demeanor was calm as they began the conversation, but as Detective Thompson presented their evidence, a flicker of unease crossed her face. "I don't know what you're talking about. I had nothing to do with Evan's disappearance."

Mark noticed a subtle tremor in Emily's hands as she held her coffee cup. "We're not accusing you, but we're trying to understand the connections. Evan's investigations might have triggered something that you wanted to keep hidden."

Emily's eyes darted between them, her composure wavering. "Look, I didn't like his family, but that doesn't mean I would do something like this."

The group sensed that they were close to something, that Emily's reaction might be a clue. But they knew they needed more information to make any conclusions.

As they continued their interviews with other suspects, a pattern began to emerge. Each individual had a story of discontent – a sense of missed opportunities, personal grievances, and unfulfilled desires. The investigation was revealing a town plagued by secrets and suppressed emotions, a town where envy and bitterness had festered for far too long.

With each conversation, the group saw the effects of these emotions on the suspects' behaviors. Some became defensive, others evasive, and a few exhibited signs of guilt that were difficult to ignore.

The moon was high in the sky when they finally regrouped at the Victorian house, their minds racing with the insights they had gained. Detective Thompson leaned against the table, her expression thoughtful. "It's clear that the motives behind Evan's disappearance run deep. These individuals are linked by a shared history of discontent and rivalry."

Amy nodded, her voice reflective. "They might have seen Evan's investigations as a threat, a chance for the truth to be revealed and their secrets exposed."

Daniel's voice was tinged with frustration. "All these years of grudges and hidden motives have led us to this point. We need to find a way to bring the truth to light."

As the group contemplated their next steps, they were filled with a renewed determination. The investigation had revealed the underbelly of the town – a place where happiness had been overshadowed by jealousy, where rivalry had festered, and where old wounds had never truly healed.

With each interview, each confrontation, they were drawing closer to the heart of the matter. The emotions that had driven Evan's disappearance were becoming clearer, the motives more tangible. The group knew that they were on the cusp of discovering the truth that had remained concealed for far too long. And as they prepared to face the final leg of their journey, they were resolved to see the investigation through to its conclusion, no matter how unsettling the revelations might be.

The town of Willowbrook was shrouded in darkness as the investigation pressed on, reaching a critical juncture. The group had identified suspects whose lives were tainted by jealousy and resentment, individuals who might have been driven to desperate measures to protect their secrets. With the truth within their grasp, they prepared to confront the poison of envy that had plagued the town for generations.

The living room of the Victorian house was illuminated by the soft glow of lamplight as the group reviewed their findings. Detective Thompson's voice was measured as she addressed the team. "We've seen their reactions, we've felt the weight of their emotions. Now, it's time to confront our suspects and see if we can unmask the truth."

Mark's gaze was unwavering. "We need to be prepared for anything. These individuals might react in unexpected ways, especially if they feel cornered."

Amy added, "Our goal is to get them to reveal their true motives. We'll be looking for any signs of guilt or unease."

With their plan in place, they set out to confront the suspects one by one. Their first stop was the home of James Harrison, a man with a history of conflicts with Evan's family. As they approached the front door, a sense of anticipation hung in the air.

James greeted them with a mix of surprise and suspicion. Detective Thompson explained their purpose, detailing the connections they had uncovered and the motives that might have driven him to silence Evan.

James's expression darkened, his voice edged with defensiveness. "You're accusing me of something I didn't do. I had no reason to hurt Evan."

Daniel leaned forward, his gaze unwavering. "We're not accusing you, but we're trying to understand what might have happened that night."

As the conversation continued, the group watched for any signs of guilt – shifts in body language, inconsistencies in James's story, or a slip of the tongue. But despite their careful observations, James's demeanor remained guarded.

Their next stop was Emily Montgomery's residence. As they presented their evidence and theories, her initial composure wavered. She became defensive, her voice tinged with frustration. "I don't know where you're getting this from. I didn't do anything to Evan."

Amy observed the tension in the room, the way Emily's eyes darted and her hands trembled. But they needed more than just unease – they needed something concrete, a revelation that would unmask the truth.

The final confrontation was with David Montgomery, a man whose family had a long history of conflicts with the Harrisons. As the group presented their case, David's expressions shifted – from surprise to anger, and finally to resignation.

"I didn't want to do it," David admitted, his voice filled with remorse. "But I felt like I had to protect my family's reputation. Evan was digging into things that we've kept hidden for years."

The room was filled with a heavy silence as David recounted his actions – how jealousy and resentment had driven him to

desperate measures. The poison of envy had corroded his judgment, leading to a choice that he would forever regret.
As the truth emerged, the group felt a mix of sadness and relief. The mystery that had haunted them for days was finally unraveled, the motives laid bare.

The moon was still high in the sky as they regrouped in the living room, the weight of their investigation settling upon them. Detective Thompson's voice was reflective. "Envy has a way of poisoning relationships, of leading people to make choices they might never have considered otherwise."

Daniel nodded, his expression somber. "This town has been haunted by envy and rivalry for far too long. It's time for the truth to be brought into the light."

With the case closed, the group knew that their journey was far from over. The poison of envy had left scars on the town, scars that would take time to heal. But with the truth now known, Willowbrook could begin the process of moving forward, of confronting its history and the darkness that had been concealed for generations.

As the moon began to wane, its light served as a reminder – a reminder that even in the darkest of times, the truth has the power to shine through, to dispel the shadows, and to bring justice to those who had been wronged.

PLAYING GAMES WITH DEATH

The sun began to rise over Willowbrook, casting a warm glow over the town. With the truth about Evan's disappearance finally revealed, the group found themselves reflecting on the events that had led them to this point. As they gathered in the living room of the Victorian house, a new realization began to take shape – the significance of the party games that had been played on that fateful evening.

Detective Thompson's voice was thoughtful as she addressed the group. "We've learned about the hidden motives, the rivalry, and the poison of envy that has plagued this town. But there's still one piece of the puzzle that we need to explore – the party games that were played at Daniel's birthday celebration."

Amy nodded, her gaze focused. "Those games might hold clues that we haven't fully considered. They were a part of the evening, and they could have some connection to what happened later."

Mark leaned over the table, his expression curious. "Let's review the details of the games – the participants, the rules, everything. Maybe there's something that we missed, something that could shed light on the events that transpired."

As they began to delve into the significance of the party games, they realized that each game had a unique context that could provide insights into the dynamics of the group and the emotions that had been simmering beneath the surface.

"The game of 'Trust or Dare'," Sarah mused. "That was the one where participants had to choose between revealing a secret or taking on a dare. It was meant to be lighthearted, but given what we know now, it could have taken on a more sinister meaning."

Daniel's voice was contemplative. "Maybe someone revealed a secret that they didn't want Evan to know. Or maybe Evan himself uncovered something during the game."

The group revisited the memories of that evening, piecing together the conversations and interactions that had taken place during the games. The laughter, the tension, and the secrets that had been shared all took on new significance in light of what they had learned.

Detective Thompson's gaze was focused, her voice steady. "We need to talk to everyone who was present at the party, especially those who participated in the games. Their perspectives might help us uncover any connections between the games and Evan's disappearance."

The group set out to interview the partygoers once more, seeking to understand the context of the party games and whether they held any clues to the events that had unfolded later in the evening.

As they listened to the participants' accounts, a new layer of complexity emerged. Stories of dares that pushed boundaries, secrets that were revealed, and tensions that simmered beneath the surface began to intertwine with the town's history and the motives they had uncovered.

One partygoer, Lisa, recounted a dare that involved entering the abandoned factory alone. She mentioned that Evan had accompanied her, sharing a fascination with exploring hidden places.

"Evan was always curious, always willing to go where others wouldn't," Lisa said, her voice tinged with nostalgia. "I had forgotten about that until now."
The realization hit the group like a jolt – the abandoned factory, the hidden treasure, and Evan's relentless pursuit of the truth. The party games had been a microcosm of the larger narrative, a reflection of the tensions and rivalries that had festered within the town.
As they pieced together the significance of the party games, the group understood that the events of that evening had been a culmination of emotions that had been building for years. The games had provided an opportunity for hidden motives to surface, for secrets to be shared, and for tensions to escalate. With each conversation, they gained a deeper understanding of the connections between the games, the town's history, and Evan's investigation. The games had acted as a catalyst, a way for the poison of envy and the weight of rivalries to come to the surface, ultimately leading to a tragic outcome.
As the sun rose higher in the sky, the group knew that their journey was nearing its end. The truth had been uncovered, the motives laid bare, and the town's history confronted. The party games had served as a lens through which they had unraveled the complexities of the human heart – its desires, its fears, and its capacity for both good and evil.
With a sense of closure, the group was prepared to bring their investigation to a conclusion. The puzzle had been solved, the shadows dispelled, and the town of Willowbrook could now begin the process of healing, knowing that the truth had finally been brought to light.
The days in Willowbrook had taken on a different hue since the truth about Evan's disappearance had come to light. The town was no longer shrouded in mystery, but instead, it was grappling with the revelations that had been uncovered. As the group gathered in the living room of the Victorian house, they knew that their investigation was coming to an end, but

there was one final thread they needed to explore – the significance of the party game "Truth or Dare."

Detective Thompson's gaze was reflective as she addressed the group. "We've peeled back the layers of this town's history, its rivalries, and the motivations behind Evan's disappearance. But the party games hold a key to understanding the emotions that were at play on the night of Daniel's birthday."

Amy nodded, her expression thoughtful. "The games served as a way for hidden truths and desires to surface. They might have provided a moment of vulnerability, a glimpse into the hearts of the partygoers."

Mark leaned forward, his voice measured. "Let's review the specific instances of 'Truth or Dare' and see if we can extract any connections to the events that followed."

As they revisited the accounts of the partygoers, they began to see how the game had acted as a conduit for emotions that had been simmering beneath the surface.

"The dare that involved going into the abandoned factory," Sarah said. "Evan and Lisa went together. It's like they were exploring the unknown, seeking something hidden."

Daniel's voice was thoughtful. "And that hidden treasure – it became a metaphor for the truths that people wanted to keep concealed."

With a renewed sense of purpose, they set out to interview the partygoers once more, this time focusing on their experiences during the game of "Truth or Dare." Their goal was to understand the emotional context of the game and whether any confessions or desires had been revealed that night.

As they spoke to the participants, a complex tapestry of emotions began to emerge. Some admitted to sharing secrets that they had never revealed before, while others spoke of dares that pushed their boundaries and brought hidden desires to the surface.

One partygoer, Alex, recounted a truth that had been shared during the game. "Someone admitted to holding a grudge against Evan's family for something that had happened years ago. It was a moment of vulnerability that no one expected."
Detective Thompson's eyes lit up with recognition. "That grudge might have played a role in the events that followed – the escalation of tensions and the eventual confrontation."
Mark added, "The truths and desires that were exposed during the game might have acted as triggers, fueling the emotions that led to Evan's disappearance."
With each conversation, the group gained a deeper understanding of how the game had acted as a catalyst, setting the stage for the conflicts and confrontations that would define the rest of the evening. The emotions that had been brought to light during "Truth or Dare" had laid the groundwork for the tragedy that had unfolded later that night.
As the interviews came to an end, the group sat in contemplative silence, their minds filled with the weight of what they had uncovered. The party games had provided a glimpse into the darkness that could reside within the human heart – the envy, the desires, and the secrets that could lead to devastating consequences.
With a sense of closure, the group realized that their investigation had come full circle. The truth had been revealed, the motivations understood, and the town's history confronted. The party games had acted as a lens through which they had explored the complexities of human nature – its vulnerabilities, its flaws, and its capacity for both connection and conflict.
As they looked out of the window at the town of Willowbrook, they knew that its healing had begun. The shadows of the past had been exposed, and now it was time for the town to move forward, armed with the knowledge that

the truth could bring both closure and the possibility of redemption.

The sun hung low on the horizon, casting long shadows over Willowbrook. The town was no longer the same – the secrets had been revealed, the motives uncovered, and the truth laid bare. As the group gathered in the living room of the Victorian house, there was a sense of finality in the air. They had journeyed through a maze of history, rivalries, and hidden desires, and now it was time to confront the last piece of the puzzle – the connection between the party games and the murder of Evan.

Detective Thompson's voice was resolute as she addressed the group. "We've explored every facet of this case, but the games that were played on the night of Daniel's birthday still hold a significance we need to understand."

Amy nodded, her expression focused. "Those games might have provided the spark that ignited the series of events leading to Evan's disappearance. We need to examine the emotions and dynamics that the games brought to the surface."

Mark leaned over the table, his voice measured. "Let's go back to that evening – the party, the games, the conversations. We need to piece together the moments that led to the tragedy."

As they reviewed their notes and memories, they began to see how the party games had acted as a microcosm of the tensions that had been building within the group.

"The 'Trust or Dare' game," Sarah said. "It revealed secrets and vulnerabilities, but it might have also intensified rivalries and exposed hidden motives."

Daniel's voice was heavy with realization. "And the game involving the abandoned factory – it's like we were exploring the unknown, just like Evan was exploring the town's history."

With their insights in mind, they set out to interview the partygoers again, this time focusing on the connections between the games and the events that had unfolded later that

night. Their goal was to understand how the games had shaped the interactions and emotions, leading to the confrontation that had ultimately resulted in Evan's death.
As they spoke to the participants, a pattern began to emerge. The "Truth or Dare" game had revealed insecurities, secrets, and grudges that had fueled the tension throughout the evening. The game involving the abandoned factory had stoked Evan's curiosity, driving him to uncover truths that others wanted to keep hidden.
One partygoer, Jake, spoke of a dare that had involved confronting someone with an unspoken grievance. "It was meant to be a joke, but it escalated into a heated argument. It was like the games were stirring up emotions that had been bubbling beneath the surface."
Detective Thompson's eyes lit up as she connected the dots. "The games were like a pressure cooker, intensifying emotions and bringing hidden conflicts to light. It was the perfect storm that set the stage for the confrontation."
With each interview, the group gained a deeper understanding of how the party games had set the tone for the evening's events. The emotions that had been stirred during the games had acted as a fuse, leading to a confrontation that had spiraled out of control.
As the sun dipped below the horizon, casting long shadows over the town, the group sat in silence, absorbing the weight of their discoveries. The twisted celebrations, the games that had exposed vulnerabilities and desires, had led to a tragedy that had shattered the lives of everyone involved.
With a sense of closure, they realized that their journey had come to an end. The town of Willowbrook had been forever changed by the revelations, but now it had the opportunity to heal, to confront its past, and to learn from the mistakes that had led to such a devastating outcome.
As they prepared to leave the living room, the group knew that the truth had been unveiled – the truth about the games,

the rivalries, and the motivations that had driven the events of that night. And as they stepped out into the cool evening air, they carried with them the knowledge that the darkness of the past could give way to the possibility of redemption and growth.

THE CRYPTIC MESSAGES

Willowbrook's streets were quiet as the sun began to set, casting a warm glow over the town. The truth about Evan's disappearance had been uncovered, but there was still one lingering mystery that captured the group's attention – the cryptic notes and symbols that had been found throughout the investigation. As they gathered in the living room of the Victorian house, they knew that unraveling this final puzzle could shed even more light on the events that had transpired.

Detective Thompson's gaze was focused as she addressed the group. "We've learned about the history, the rivalries, and the emotions that fueled Evan's investigation. But the cryptic notes and symbols might hold a key to understanding the intricate web of connections."

Amy nodded, her expression thoughtful. "These notes were more than just random occurrences. They were deliberate, and they might have a deeper meaning that we haven't fully grasped."

Mark leaned forward, his voice contemplative. "Let's review the notes we've collected – the ones found at the factory, the party, and other locations. Maybe they'll reveal a pattern or provide insight into the motivations behind them."

As they examined the notes and symbols, they began to see a common thread – a trail of clues that had been left behind like breadcrumbs, waiting to be deciphered.

"The note found at the abandoned factory," Sarah said. "It mentioned 'unearthing the past' and 'revealing the truth.' It's like whoever left it knew what was about to happen."

Daniel's voice was filled with intrigue. "And the symbols that were painted on the walls – they seemed to correspond to different locations in town."

With a renewed sense of purpose, they set out to analyze the notes and symbols in greater detail. They considered the context in which each note had been discovered, the locations they referred to, and the connections to the town's history.

"The note found at the party," Detective Thompson mused. "It mentioned 'hidden treasure' and 'long-buried secrets.' It's like whoever wrote it was aware of the tensions that existed."

Mark added, "And the symbols might have been a way of signaling to someone – a secret language that only a select few understood."

With their insights in mind, they revisited the locations mentioned in the notes, searching for additional clues that might tie everything together. They combed through the history of the town, seeking connections between the notes, the symbols, and the individuals who had been involved.

One evening, as they gathered around the table covered in notes and maps, a breakthrough occurred. Amy's eyes lit up as she pointed to a series of symbols that had been repeated in various locations. "These symbols – they're not random. They seem to represent the initials of key individuals."

Detective Thompson's gaze sharpened. "Initials of individuals who were somehow connected to Evan's investigation?"

As they continued to analyze the symbols and their connections to the town's history, a pattern emerged. The symbols corresponded to individuals who had played a role in the events leading to Evan's disappearance – the Montgomerys, the Harrisons, and others who had been intertwined in the town's web of secrets.

With each revelation, the group's excitement grew. The cryptic notes and symbols had been a trail of clues, a way of pointing them toward the heart of the mystery. It was as if someone had been orchestrating a series of breadcrumbs, leading them to the truth that had been concealed for so long.

As they pieced together the connections, they realized that the cryptic notes and symbols had been a silent narrator, guiding them through the twists and turns of the investigation. The notes had revealed a deep understanding of the town's history, the motivations behind the events, and the desires that had driven individuals to extreme actions.

As the sun set, bathing the room in a warm, golden light, the group sat back in their chairs, a sense of satisfaction settling over them. The trail of clues had been followed, the puzzle had been solved, and the town's secrets had been laid bare. The cryptic notes and symbols, like whispers from the past, had led them to the truth – a truth that was both intricate and haunting, a truth that had finally been brought into the light.

The town of Willowbrook was bathed in the soft glow of morning as a new day began. The group had journeyed through the twists and turns of Evan's disappearance, uncovering secrets, motives, and the truth that had long remained concealed. But there was still one puzzle that remained – the meaning behind the cryptic notes and symbols that had guided them through the investigation. As they gathered in the living room of the Victorian house, they knew that they were on the cusp of understanding the full story.

Detective Thompson's voice was filled with anticipation as she addressed the group. "We've followed the trail of clues left by the cryptic notes and symbols. Now, it's time to piece together the final message they hold."

Amy nodded, her gaze focused. "These notes were like a puzzle, each piece leading us closer to the truth. We need to consider the connections between the symbols and the individuals they correspond to."

Mark leaned forward, his expression determined. "Let's go back to each note and symbol and try to find the common thread that ties them all together."

As they reviewed the notes and symbols, they began to see how the puzzle was unfolding. The symbols had represented initials of key individuals – those who had played a role in the events leading to Evan's disappearance.

"The initials of the Montgomerys and the Harrisons," Sarah said. "These families had been at the center of the town's history, and their actions had a ripple effect on everyone else."

Daniel's voice was filled with insight. "The notes mentioned 'unearthing the past' and 'revealing the truth.' It's like they were guiding us to confront the history that had been buried for so long."

With their analysis in mind, they revisited the locations mentioned in the notes, seeking to understand their significance in the context of the larger narrative. Each location held a piece of the puzzle, a clue that would help them decipher the message hidden within the cryptic notes.

As they delved deeper, they realized that the notes had been strategically placed – a trail of breadcrumbs that had led them on a journey of discovery. The message they held was not just about Evan's disappearance, but about the town itself – its history, its rivalries, and the emotions that had driven its residents for generations.

Detective Thompson's eyes shone with realization. "The notes were a way of communicating a story, a narrative that had been woven through the fabric of the town. They were meant to guide us, to lead us to the heart of the mystery."

As they pieced together the connections between the notes, symbols, and individuals, a coherent picture emerged. The puzzle had been solved, and the message it conveyed was clear – a story of jealousy, rivalries, and long-buried secrets that had festered over time.

With a sense of completion, the group sat back in their chairs, the weight of their discoveries settling over them. The puzzle had unfolded, revealing a narrative that was both haunting and illuminating. The cryptic notes and symbols had served as a guiding light, leading them to the truth that had remained hidden for so long.

As the morning sun continued to rise, the group knew that their journey was coming to an end. The town of Willowbrook had been forever changed by their investigation, and now it had the opportunity to heal, to confront its past, and to learn from its mistakes.

With a final glance at the notes and symbols that had led them on this intricate journey, the group left the living room, carrying with them the knowledge that even the most cryptic of messages can be deciphered when approached with patience, determination, and a willingness to uncover the truth.

The sun hung low in the sky over Willowbrook, casting long shadows as the town grappled with the aftermath of the revelations. The investigation into Evan's disappearance had uncovered the truth, but there was still one element that eluded the group's grasp – the identity of the killer. As they gathered in the living room of the Victorian house, they knew that they were about to embark on a final, intense phase of the investigation – following the killer's taunting leads.

Detective Thompson's gaze was resolute as she addressed the group. "We've uncovered the history, the rivalries, and the motivations behind Evan's disappearance. But the killer is still out there, and they've left us a trail of taunting leads to follow."

Amy nodded, her expression determined. "The cryptic notes and symbols were like a game to the killer, a way of challenging us to uncover their identity. We need to analyze these leads carefully and see if they can guide us to the truth."

Mark leaned forward, his voice resolute. "Let's revisit the notes and symbols and try to decipher the intentions behind them. The killer might have left behind clues that reveal their thought process."

As they reviewed the leads, they began to see a pattern of taunting and challenge. The killer had orchestrated a cat-and-mouse game, leaving cryptic messages that were meant to draw them deeper into the mystery.

"The notes were deliberately placed in locations that held significance," Sarah observed. "The killer wanted us to revisit these places, to understand the connections they had to Evan's investigation."

Daniel's voice was tinged with frustration. "It's like the killer was always one step ahead, watching our every move and manipulating our actions."

With a renewed determination, they set out to analyze each lead in detail. They considered the context in which the notes were found, the symbols that had been painted, and the individuals they corresponded to. Each lead was like a thread, connecting the killer's actions to the larger narrative.

As they delved deeper, they realized that the leads were not just random acts of taunting – they were a way for the killer to communicate their knowledge of the investigation and their desire to remain hidden.

Detective Thompson's eyes narrowed as a realization struck her. "The leads might also serve as a distraction, a way of diverting our attention from the real motive and the true identity of the killer."

Amy added, "By focusing on these taunting leads, we might be missing something that's right in front of us – a clue that reveals the killer's true intentions."

With their insights in mind, they revisited the locations mentioned in the leads, seeking to uncover any hidden connections or overlooked details. The chase had become intense, a race against time to decipher the clues and unmask the killer before they could slip away.

As they pieced together the puzzle of the taunting leads, they understood that this phase of the investigation was unlike any other. The killer was no longer just a shadow – they were an active participant, a manipulator who reveled in the game they had created.

With each lead followed, each clue deciphered, the group grew closer to the truth. The cat-and-mouse chase had intensified, but they were determined to stay one step ahead of the killer, to outwit their cunning and bring their reign of terror to an end.

As the sun began to dip below the horizon, casting long shadows over the town, the group left the living room with a sense of urgency. The taunting leads had set them on a path of challenge and danger, but they were resolute in their pursuit. The chase had begun, and they were determined to follow it to its conclusion – to unveil the identity of the killer and finally bring justice to Evan and the town of Willowbrook.

A MIDNIGHT VISITOR

The moon hung high in the sky over Willowbrook, casting an eerie glow over the town. The investigation into Evan's disappearance had reached a critical juncture as the group continued to follow the killer's taunting leads. But there was a palpable tension in the air – a feeling that they were being watched, that the chase had taken a dangerous turn. As they gathered in the living room of the Victorian house, they knew that an unsettling encounter awaited them – an encounter with the intruder who had been orchestrating this deadly game.

Detective Thompson's voice was stern as she addressed the group. "We're close to uncovering the killer's identity, but we need to be prepared for anything. The notes and symbols have led us to this point, and the encounter with the intruder could hold vital information."

Amy nodded, her expression cautious. "We can't underestimate their cunning. They've manipulated the investigation at every turn, and now they might be trying to confront us directly."

Mark leaned forward, his voice resolute. "Let's ensure our safety and approach this encounter with caution. We need to gather as much information as possible without putting ourselves in danger."

With a sense of anticipation, they made their way through the town, guided by the leads that the killer had left behind. The night was quiet, the streets empty, but there was an unease in the air – a feeling that they were not alone.

As they reached the location indicated by the final lead, a chill ran down their spines. The abandoned factory loomed before them, its dark windows and creaking doors hinting at the secrets it held.

Detective Thompson's voice was steady. "Stay close and be vigilant. We don't know what we're walking into."

As they cautiously entered the factory, their flashlights pierced the darkness, revealing a labyrinth of shadows and forgotten memories. The echoes of their footsteps seemed to bounce off the walls, a reminder that they were not alone.

Suddenly, a noise echoed through the factory – a distant footstep, a rustling of metal. The group tensed, their senses on high alert as they tried to pinpoint the source of the sound.

And then, in the beam of a flashlight, a figure appeared – a shadowy silhouette that seemed to materialize out of thin air.

"Welcome," a voice echoed, dripping with a chilling amusement.

As their flashlights illuminated the intruder's face, a wave of recognition washed over them. It was someone they knew, someone who had been present throughout their investigation.

The intruder's lips curled into a smile, a smile that held a mixture of arrogance and satisfaction. "Impressive, isn't it? The puzzle, the chase – it was all part of the plan."

Amy's voice was edged with frustration. "You orchestrated this entire game, taunting us, leading us on a wild goose chase."

The intruder's smile widened. "But it wasn't just a game. It was a way of forcing you to confront the truths that you'd rather keep hidden."

Mark's expression darkened. "You're responsible for Evan's disappearance. You're the one who left the cryptic notes and symbols."

The intruder's laughter echoed through the factory, bouncing off the walls like a haunting melody. "You're getting closer, but the truth is still just out of reach."

With those words, the intruder turned and disappeared into the shadows, leaving the group standing in the darkness, their hearts pounding with a mixture of frustration and determination.

As they regrouped in the moonlit night, the group knew that they were closer than ever to unmasking the killer's identity. The encounter had been unsettling, a reminder of the danger that lurked in the shadows. But they were determined to press forward, to follow the trail of clues that had been laid before them and finally bring an end to this deadly game.

With the moon as their witness, they left the abandoned factory, their flashlights cutting through the darkness as they continued their pursuit. The footsteps in the dark had led them to an encounter they would not soon forget, an encounter that had brought them face to face with the one who had orchestrated this intricate, deadly dance.

The night hung heavy over Willowbrook, shrouding the town in darkness. The group had come face to face with the intruder, a manipulator who had orchestrated the cryptic notes, symbols, and taunting leads. The chase had escalated, and they knew that they were on the brink of a final confrontation – a deadly game of hide and seek that would determine the fate of Evan's investigation. As they gathered in the living room of the Victorian house, tension hummed in the air, and a sense of urgency settled over them.

Detective Thompson's voice was resolute as she addressed the group. "The encounter with the intruder confirmed that we're on the right track. But we need to proceed with caution. This is a dangerous game, and we can't afford any missteps."

Amy nodded, her expression determined. "The killer wants us to confront them, to unravel the truth. We need to stay focused and gather all the information we can before we make our move."

Mark leaned forward, his voice firm. "Let's analyze the clues we have and see if we can predict the killer's next move. We can't let them outmaneuver us."

As they reviewed the leads, notes, and symbols, they began to piece together a pattern – a narrative that the killer had carefully constructed, leading them to this moment.

"The killer's motivations are rooted in the history of the town," Sarah said. "The notes and symbols were like a trail of breadcrumbs, guiding us through the past and present."

Daniel's voice was determined. "The killer wants us to confront the truth, to expose their actions and motivations. It's like they're playing a deadly game of hide and seek, daring us to find them."

With their analysis complete, they set out to decipher the final clue – the one that would lead them to the killer's lair. The moon cast long shadows as they navigated the town's streets, their senses heightened as they followed the breadcrumbs that had been left behind.

As they reached the location indicated by the final clue, an abandoned building stood before them – a haunting silhouette against the night sky.

Detective Thompson's voice was steady. "We know the killer is here. Stay alert and be prepared for anything."

They entered the building cautiously, their flashlights sweeping the darkness as they ventured deeper. The air was thick with tension, and the echoes of their footsteps seemed to reverberate through the space.

And then, in a flicker of movement, a figure emerged from the shadows – the intruder, their face illuminated by the soft glow of a single light.

"Congratulations," the intruder's voice echoed, laced with a mixture of mockery and defiance. "You've followed the trail and uncovered the truth. But can you handle the final revelation?"

Amy's voice was resolute. "You can't hide any longer. Your game is over."

The intruder's laughter echoed through the building, chilling the air. "Oh, but the game has only just begun. You see, I have one final challenge for you."

As the intruder spoke, a series of screens lit up around them, displaying images, symbols, and connections that seemed to weave together the town's history and the killer's motivations.

"This is your last chance," the intruder taunted. "Can you decipher the connections? Can you unravel the truth that has been concealed for so long?"

With a surge of determination, the group focused on the screens, analyzing the information before them. The images and symbols seemed to come together like pieces of a jigsaw puzzle, revealing a larger picture.

As they pieced together the connections, a realization dawned – the identity of the killer, the motivations behind their actions, and the truth that had been hidden beneath layers of deception.

Detective Thompson's voice was unwavering. "We know who you are. Your secrets are no longer safe."

The intruder's face contorted with a mixture of anger and desperation. "You may have unraveled my puzzle, but you can't change the past. It's too late for that."

As the words hung in the air, the intruder vanished into the darkness, leaving the group standing in the aftermath of the confrontation. The deadly game of hide and seek had reached its climax, and now they were armed with the knowledge they needed to finally bring justice to Evan and the town of Willowbrook.

With the moon as their witness, they left the abandoned building, the night air carrying the weight of their discoveries. The confrontation had been intense, a battle of wits and wills that had brought them closer to the truth. The shadows may have concealed the killer's actions, but now they were prepared to shine a light on the darkness and uncover the final piece of the puzzle.

The night was fraught with tension in Willowbrook, a town haunted by the shadows of its past. The group had confronted the killer and unraveled the intricate puzzle they had laid out, but the danger was far from over. As they reconvened in the living room of the Victorian house, they knew that they had to remain vigilant, for the killer's grasp extended beyond their encounter – and the chase was not yet concluded.

Detective Thompson's voice was resolute as she addressed the group. "We've identified the killer and exposed their motivations, but they won't rest until their secrets remain hidden. We need to ensure our safety and put an end to this deadly game."

Amy nodded, her expression determined. "The killer may be desperate now that their plan is unraveling. We need to be cautious and anticipate their next move."

Mark leaned forward, his voice firm. "Let's stay ahead of them. We know their identity and their motivations. Now, we must strategize to escape their clutches and bring them to justice."

As they reviewed the evidence and analyzed the puzzle they had deciphered, they began to see the killer's pattern of manipulation and deception.

"The killer used the notes, symbols, and the confrontation to control the narrative," Sarah said. "They wanted to guide our perceptions and emotions."

Daniel's voice was resolute. "But now that we see through their web of lies, we can anticipate their tactics and stay one step ahead."

With their insights in mind, they set out to fortify their defenses and plan their next move. They knew that the killer wouldn't relent, and they had to be prepared for whatever challenges lay ahead.

As the moon hung high in the sky, casting long shadows over the town, they gathered the evidence, secured their living quarters, and devised a strategy to protect themselves. They were united in their determination to escape the killer's trap and ensure their safety.

But just as they were settling in, a chilling realization struck – the killer had managed to infiltrate their safe haven.

Footsteps echoed through the house, each one carrying an ominous weight. The group tensed, their senses on high alert as they tried to pinpoint the source of the noise.

And then, in the moonlit hallway, a figure appeared – the intruder, their face obscured by darkness.

"You can't escape," the intruder's voice echoed, dripping with malice. "I've been watching, waiting for the perfect moment to strike."

Amy's voice was edged with defiance. "We're not afraid of you anymore. Your reign of terror ends here."

The intruder's laughter filled the air, a chilling sound that seemed to seep into every corner of the room. "You think you can outwit me? You're just pawns in my game."

Mark's expression hardened. "Your game is over. We've seen through your lies, your manipulation. You can't control us anymore."

With those words, the group sprang into action, using their knowledge of the killer's tactics to counter their every move. The confrontation that followed was a battle of wits and survival, a test of their determination and resilience.

As they fought to escape the killer's clutches, the group was reminded of the strength that came from their unity. Their shared purpose, their knowledge of the killer's motivations, and their unwavering resolve gave them the upper hand.

In the end, their careful planning and quick thinking paid off. The killer's hold was broken, their attempts at manipulation thwarted.

As the first light of dawn broke over the town, the group emerged from the house, their expressions marked by weariness but also a sense of victory. The escape from the killer's trap had been a harrowing ordeal, a testament to their strength and resourcefulness.

As they looked out at the town of Willowbrook, they knew that the darkness had been lifted, that the killer's reign of terror had come to an end. The shadows that had haunted the town were dissipating, and in their wake, a new chapter was beginning – one of healing, redemption, and the possibility of a brighter future.

UNMASKING THE CULPRIT

The dawn painted the skies of Willowbrook in soft hues, marking the beginning of a new day. The town was on the cusp of healing after the ordeal with the killer, yet there were still unanswered questions lingering in the air. As the group assembled in the living room of the Victorian house, they knew that unraveling the final threads of deception and misdirection was crucial for the closure they sought.

Detective Thompson's voice was resolute as she addressed the group. "The confrontation with the killer brought us closer to the truth, but there are still pieces of the puzzle that need to be uncovered. We need to untangle the web of deception that the killer wove."

Amy nodded, her expression determined. "The killer's manipulation and lies led us astray for so long. Now, armed with the knowledge of their identity, we must sort through the truth and falsehoods to find the complete story."

Mark leaned forward, his voice firm. "Let's reexamine the evidence, the statements, and the actions of those involved. By dissecting the lies and misdirection, we can piece together a clearer picture."

As they reviewed the evidence and statements, they began to identify the moments when the killer had steered them away from the truth.

"The killer exploited the town's history and tensions to create a smokescreen," Sarah observed. "They used the cryptic notes and symbols to direct our focus elsewhere."

Daniel's voice was analytical. "And during our encounters with them, they tried to control the narrative, to make us doubt our instincts and conclusions."

With a renewed determination, they set out to identify the moments when the killer had manipulated events to suit their own agenda. They meticulously pieced together timelines, cross-referenced statements, and reconstructed the series of actions that had led to Evan's disappearance.

"Remember the party," Detective Thompson said. "The killer might have been present, using misdirection to divert our attention away from their true intentions."

Amy added, "And the moments when we thought we were close to the truth – those were the moments when the killer might have been most desperate to lead us astray."

Mark's expression hardened. "We need to expose these instances of manipulation. By highlighting the lies, we can bring clarity to the investigation and finally close this chapter."

As they delved deeper, they realized that the web of deception the killer had woven was intricate and pervasive. It extended beyond the cryptic notes and symbols, infiltrating their interactions, emotions, and perceptions.

"The killer's ultimate goal was to maintain control over the narrative," Sarah noted. "They wanted to ensure that their secrets remained hidden."

Daniel's voice was filled with conviction. "But by exposing their deception, we can take that control away from them. The truth will be the ultimate revelation."

With each piece of deception exposed, the group felt a sense of clarity and closure. The lies that had clouded their judgment were being dismantled, leaving behind a foundation of truth on which to build the final resolution.

As they continued to dissect the events and interactions that had transpired, they were reminded of the importance of resilience, determination, and a commitment to uncovering the truth. The web of deception might have been complex, but their collective efforts were proving to be a powerful force against it.

With the sun rising higher in the sky, casting warm light into the living room, the group pressed on with their analysis. The web of deception was slowly being untangled, revealing the path to justice and healing that had long been obscured.

Willowbrook woke to a new day, the air carrying a sense of renewal after the darkness that had enveloped the town. The group had diligently unraveled the web of deception, bringing them closer to understanding the truth behind Evan's disappearance. But there was one crucial step left – confronting the potential murderers who had been entangled in the web of secrets. As they assembled in the living room of the Victorian house, a mix of determination and apprehension lingered in the air.

Detective Thompson's voice was resolute as she addressed the group. "We've uncovered the deception and lies that shrouded this investigation. Now, we need to gather the suspects and confront them with the truth."

Amy nodded, her expression focused. "By gathering those who may have had a motive to harm Evan, we can test their reactions and gather information that might lead us to the final pieces of the puzzle."

Mark leaned forward, his voice firm. "Let's approach this step with caution. Emotions are running high, and we need to ensure that our confrontation is focused on uncovering the truth."

As they reviewed their list of potential suspects, they began to strategize the best approach to confronting them.

"The killer's manipulation might have extended to the suspects," Sarah noted. "They could have planted seeds of doubt and misinformation to keep themselves hidden."
Daniel's voice was analytical. "We should consider each suspect's interactions, statements, and their connections to the events that transpired. By confronting them, we can gauge their reactions and potentially uncover new information."
With their plan in place, they set out to gather the suspects – individuals who had been implicated in the web of deception, who had motives that aligned with the tangled history of Willowbrook.
As they met with each suspect, their conversations were measured, guided by their knowledge of the deception that had been at play. They probed for reactions, inconsistencies, and any hints that might lead them closer to the truth.
"The confrontation is about challenging their versions of events," Detective Thompson said. "By comparing their accounts with what we know, we can uncover any gaps or contradictions."
Amy added, "We need to keep our emotions in check and remain focused on the goal – to gather information that will help us complete the puzzle."
Mark's expression was unwavering. "Our collective determination is our strength. By presenting a united front, we can encourage the suspects to reveal what they know."
As they spoke with each suspect, their interactions were intense and revealing. The suspects were confronted with the web of deception that had been woven around them, forced to reckon with their own actions and the implications of their involvement.
The group's determination to uncover the truth was a powerful force, and it pushed the suspects to confront their own lies and evasions. With each conversation, the puzzle pieces fell into place, revealing connections and motivations that had been hidden beneath the surface.

As the day wore on, the group's encounters with the suspects yielded valuable insights. Their determination to confront the potential murderers had brought them closer to the final truth, shedding light on the events that had led to Evan's disappearance.

With the sun beginning to set, the group gathered once again in the living room, their expressions marked by a mix of weariness and resolution. The confrontations had been intense, but they had yielded important information that would help them complete the investigation.

As they reviewed their findings, they knew that the pieces of the puzzle were finally coming together. The confrontation with the suspects had been a pivotal step, and now they were prepared to use the information they had gathered to uncover the ultimate truth and bring justice to Evan and the town of Willowbrook.

The sun dipped below the horizon, casting a warm, golden glow over Willowbrook. The town had weathered the storm of deception, manipulation, and danger, and now it stood on the threshold of truth and justice. The group had tirelessly pursued the threads of the investigation, confronting suspects, and untangling the web of lies. As they gathered one last time in the living room of the Victorian house, they knew that the time had come for the final reveal – to expose the birthday boy's killer and bring an end to the mystery that had gripped the town.

Detective Thompson's voice was resolute as she addressed the group. "We've pieced together the puzzle, confronted the suspects, and uncovered the truth that had long been concealed. Now, we stand on the brink of revealing the identity of Evan's killer."

Amy nodded, her expression determined. "The killer can't escape the weight of their actions any longer. By presenting the evidence we've gathered, we can expose their motivations and finally bring closure to this tragic story."

Mark leaned forward, his voice firm. "Let's ensure that our presentation is meticulous and well-prepared. This is the moment that will bring the truth to light, and we must do it with precision."

As they reviewed the evidence, timelines, and motivations, they began to craft their presentation – a narrative that would connect the dots and lead to the ultimate revelation.

"The killer's actions were calculated," Sarah noted. "Their manipulation and misdirection were aimed at protecting themselves from the consequences of their deeds."

Daniel's voice was filled with conviction. "But now that we've unraveled their web of lies, we can expose their true nature and the extent of their involvement."

With their presentation finalized, they set out to gather the town's residents – those who had been directly impacted by the events that had transpired, and those who had a stake in the truth.

As they addressed the gathered crowd, their voices steady and resolute, they presented the evidence that had been meticulously gathered – the notes, symbols, leads, and confrontations that had led them to this moment.

"We have followed the path of deception to uncover the motivations behind Evan's disappearance," Detective Thompson said. "The killer's actions were driven by jealousy, rivalries, and a desire to protect their own secrets."

Amy added, "The cryptic notes and symbols were a way for the killer to manipulate events, to control the narrative, and to divert our attention from their true intentions."

Mark's voice was unwavering. "But through our determination and persistence, we have unveiled the truth. The killer's lies can no longer stand in the way of justice."

As the evidence was presented, the crowd's reactions ranged from shock to realization. The pieces of the puzzle were fitting into place, revealing a narrative that had remained hidden for far too long.

And then, in the hushed aftermath of their presentation, the killer's face was illuminated by a single light. The weight of the evidence and the crowd's reaction seemed to bear down on them.

"It's over," the killer's voice quivered, a mixture of defiance and resignation. "You've won."

Amy's voice was unwavering. "Your reign of manipulation and deception is finished. The truth is out, and justice will be served."

The moment was charged with emotion as the town absorbed the truth and confronted the reality of the killer's actions. The web of lies that had ensnared them was now unraveling, leaving behind a sense of closure and resolution.

As the sun set and darkness blanketed the town, the group left the living room, knowing that the final reveal had brought the truth to light. The mystery of Evan's disappearance had been solved, and the town of Willowbrook could begin the process of healing and moving forward, leaving the shadows of the past behind.

MOTIVES LAID BARE

As the days grew longer in Willowbrook, the town was finally emerging from the grip of the mystery that had plagued it for so long. The truth behind Evan's disappearance had been exposed, and justice was in motion. Yet, there was still a need to understand the motivations and justifications of the culprit, to delve into the depths of their mind and uncover the twisted logic that had driven them to commit such a heinous act. As the group gathered in the living room of the Victorian house, they prepared to confront the killer once more – not for the pursuit of truth, but for the sake of closure and understanding.

Detective Thompson's voice was measured as she addressed the group. "The evidence has revealed the truth, but now we must attempt to understand the reasoning behind the killer's actions. We need to hear their justifications and motivations, no matter how twisted they may be."

Amy nodded, her expression composed. "By allowing the culprit to speak, we can gain insight into their mindset and the events that led to this tragedy."

Mark leaned forward, his voice calm. "Let's approach this with empathy. We're seeking to understand, not to justify or excuse their actions."

With a sense of purpose, they prepared to confront the culprit – the individual who had orchestrated the deception and manipulation that had torn the town apart.

As the group faced the culprit, their expressions were a mix of determination and curiosity. They were prepared to listen, to give the culprit a chance to share their perspective.

The culprit's voice was tinged with bitterness and defiance. "You think you know everything? You have no idea what I've been through."

Amy's voice was steady. "We're here to understand. To hear your side of the story."

The culprit's words poured forth, a tale of perceived injustices, resentments, and grudges that had festered over time. They spoke of betrayal, of dreams shattered, and of a desperate need for revenge.

As the story unfolded, it became clear that the culprit's actions had been driven by a toxic mix of jealousy, anger, and a desire to regain a sense of control.

Mark's voice was empathetic. "You believed that by orchestrating Evan's disappearance, you could somehow reclaim what you felt had been taken from you."

The culprit's expression was haunted, a glimpse into the depths of their troubled mind. "I wanted them to suffer like I did. To experience the pain of loss and betrayal."

Detective Thompson's voice was compassionate. "But revenge only perpetuates the cycle of pain. It doesn't heal wounds or bring solace."

The culprit's voice softened, revealing a hint of remorse. "I see that now. I thought I could find satisfaction in their suffering, but all it brought was more pain."

As the conversation continued, the group listened without judgment, seeking to understand the complicated motivations that had led to this tragic event.

Sarah's voice was gentle. "Sometimes, our perceptions can be clouded by our emotions. Revenge might seem like a solution, but it only deepens the wounds for everyone involved."

Daniel added, "In seeking revenge, we lose sight of our own humanity and the impact our actions have on others."

The conversation was a tense and emotional journey into the mind of the culprit – a journey that revealed the complexities of human emotions, the destructive power of unchecked resentments, and the importance of breaking free from the cycle of vengeance.

As the conversation came to an end, the room was filled with a heavy silence. The group had gained insight into the culprit's motivations, but there were no easy answers or solutions.

With a final nod, the culprit left the room, leaving the group to grapple with the weight of the revelations. The tales of revenge had laid bare the destructive consequences of unchecked anger and the tragedy that had resulted from it. As they gathered their thoughts, they knew that the journey toward healing and closure was far from over. The town of Willowbrook had faced the darkness head-on, and now, as the sun began to set, they were left with the task of rebuilding and moving forward, guided by the lessons they had learned from the tales of revenge.

In the wake of the revelations and conversations that had unfolded, Willowbrook was left to grapple with the aftermath of the tragedy that had rocked the town. The group had delved into the mind of the culprit, seeking to understand the motivations and justifications that had led to Evan's disappearance. As they gathered in the living room of the Victorian house once again, they turned their focus toward the emotional triggers that had driven the events that had unfolded.

Detective Thompson's voice was thoughtful as she addressed the group. "Understanding the emotional triggers behind the actions is crucial for comprehending the depth of despair that can lead to such acts. We need to explore the circumstances that pushed the culprit to their breaking point."

Amy nodded, her expression contemplative. "By examining the emotional context, we can gain insight into the pressures and struggles that contributed to the tragedy."

Mark leaned forward, his voice empathetic. "Let's approach this with sensitivity. We're attempting to comprehend the complex emotions that can lead someone down a dark path." As they reviewed the events that had transpired, they began to piece together the emotional triggers that had played a role in the unfolding tragedy.

"The culprit's feelings of betrayal and loss were powerful catalysts," Sarah observed. "Their emotions were intensified by their perception of being wronged by those they trusted." Daniel's voice was reflective. "Desperation can cloud judgment and lead to irrational decisions. It's essential to consider the emotional turmoil that was brewing beneath the surface."

With their insights in mind, they set out to explore the events that had preceded Evan's disappearance – the moments that had triggered a sequence of emotions that ultimately led to tragedy.

"The town's history of rivalries and conflicts could have contributed to a sense of isolation and hopelessness," Detective Thompson noted. "Those feelings might have been exacerbated by personal struggles and setbacks."

Amy added, "The combination of personal and communal pressures could have created a perfect storm of desperation."

Mark's expression was solemn. "It's a reminder that we must address the underlying issues that contribute to such emotions. The town needs healing and support to prevent history from repeating itself."

As they discussed the emotional triggers, they realized that the events that had transpired were not isolated incidents. The culmination of years of unresolved issues and simmering tensions had played a significant role in pushing the culprit to their breaking point.

Sarah's voice was filled with compassion. "It's a lesson in the importance of recognizing the signs of desperation and reaching out to those who might be struggling."

Daniel added, "Desperation and despair can affect anyone, and understanding the emotional triggers can help us intervene and offer support."

The conversation was a somber exploration of the human psyche and the factors that could lead someone to commit actions they might not otherwise consider. The group's commitment to understanding the emotional context was a testament to their determination to prevent future tragedies. As the sun dipped below the horizon, casting a gentle light over the town, the group left the living room, their thoughts weighed down by the depth of emotions that they had explored. The understanding of the emotional triggers that had driven the events served as a sobering reminder of the importance of empathy, compassion, and community support in the face of desperation and despair.

Willowbrook was slowly finding its footing again, its residents grappling with the aftermath of the revelations that had shaken the town to its core. The group had navigated a journey through deception, manipulation, and tragedy, uncovering the motivations that had driven the events that had unfolded. As they gathered in the living room of the Victorian house, they turned their attention to the intricate relationship between motive and action, seeking to understand how personal motivations could lead to such devastating consequences.

Detective Thompson's voice was contemplative as she addressed the group. "Motive is a powerful force that can shape our decisions and actions. We need to delve into the impact of personal motivations on the choices people make."

Amy nodded, her expression thoughtful. "By understanding the connection between motive and action, we can gain insight into the choices that were driven by emotions, desperation, and a desire for revenge."

Mark leaned forward, his voice empathetic. "Let's consider how broken bonds and shattered relationships can warp the decisions we make, leading us down paths we might not have imagined."

As they reviewed the events that had transpired, they began to explore the motivations that had influenced the culprit's actions – the web of personal connections and emotions that had driven them to orchestrate Evan's disappearance.

"The culprit's actions were driven by a sense of betrayal," Sarah observed. "Their personal history and relationships created a motive that fueled their quest for revenge."

Daniel's voice was reflective. "Motive can cloud judgment and distort our perceptions. The strength of our emotions can lead us to make choices that we might regret later."

With their insights in mind, they set out to examine the relationships and bonds that had been broken along the way – the personal connections that had been strained by jealousy, resentment, and the pursuit of revenge.

"The town's history of conflicts and rivalries played a role in the unfolding tragedy," Detective Thompson noted. "Motive is often intertwined with our perceptions of justice and retribution."

Amy added, "The personal struggles and pressures faced by the culprit might have pushed them to take drastic actions as they sought to reclaim a sense of power and control."

Mark's expression was pensive. "It's a reminder that our decisions don't exist in isolation. The impact of broken bonds and personal motivations can ripple through a community."

As they discussed the impact of motive on action, they realized that the events that had transpired were not solely the result of an individual's choices. The town's history, relationships, and communal dynamics had all played a part in shaping the circumstances that had led to tragedy.

Sarah's voice was filled with empathy. "It's important to recognize the power of motive and to consider how our actions can affect others – sometimes in ways we never intended."

Daniel added, "Motive can be a driving force, but it's crucial to remember that we have the power to choose our actions and break the cycle of harm."

The conversation was a sobering exploration of the intricate relationship between personal motivations and the choices we make. The group's commitment to understanding the impact of broken bonds and shattered relationships was a testament to their dedication to preventing further tragedies in Willowbrook.

As the moon rose in the night sky, casting a gentle glow over the town, the group left the living room, their thoughts heavy with the weight of the connections they had explored. The understanding of the impact of motive on action served as a reminder of the importance of fostering healthy relationships, open communication, and a sense of community in order to prevent the devastating consequences of broken bonds.

PURSUIT OF JUSTICE

The winds of change swept through Willowbrook, carrying with them a mixture of healing and reflection. The group had traversed a long and arduous journey, unearthing the truth behind Evan's disappearance and the motivations that had driven the tragic events. As they gathered in the living room of the Victorian house, they turned their attention to the complex legal aspects that lay ahead – the intricate process of weighing options for prosecution and seeking justice for the crime that had shaken the town.

Detective Thompson's voice was pragmatic as she addressed the group. "We've uncovered the truth, but now we must navigate the legal landscape. Prosecution requires careful consideration of the evidence, motives, and consequences."

Amy nodded, her expression determined. "By understanding the legal chessboard, we can make informed decisions that honor both the pursuit of justice and the complexities of the human emotions that led to this tragedy."

Mark leaned forward, his voice focused. "Let's approach this step with diligence. The legal process is our avenue to ensure that the truth prevails and that accountability is upheld."

As they reviewed the evidence, motives, and their conversations with the culprit, they began to strategize the best course of action for prosecution.

"The evidence we've gathered will play a critical role," Sarah observed. "It's crucial to present a clear and compelling case that reflects the truth we've uncovered."

Daniel's voice was analytical. "We must also consider the emotional impact of the trial. The town's wounds are still fresh, and the trial could bring closure or reopen old scars." With their insights in mind, they set out to explore the different legal options available – the potential charges, trial strategies, and the implications for both the town and the culprit.

"The charges must align with the evidence and the motivations we've uncovered," Detective Thompson noted. "We need to present a case that reflects the complexity of the culprit's actions."

Amy added, "The trial will be a journey for the town as well. It's important to consider the emotional toll and ensure that justice is served while fostering healing."

Mark's expression was resolute. "Our commitment to truth and justice should guide our decisions. We must ensure that the trial offers closure and a path toward healing."

As they discussed the legal chessboard, they realized that the trial would be a pivotal moment for both the town and the individuals involved. It was a chance to bring the truth to light, to hold the culprit accountable, and to ensure that the consequences of their actions were in line with the severity of the crime.

Sarah's voice was filled with determination. "The legal process is a vital step toward closure. By upholding the principles of justice, we can ensure that the town can move forward."

Daniel added, "But let's also remember that the trial is just one part of the journey. The town's healing will extend beyond the courtroom."

The conversation was a weighty exploration of the legal process and its implications. The group's dedication to navigating the legal chessboard with integrity and compassion was a testament to their commitment to ensuring that justice was not only served, but also that the town of Willowbrook could find a path toward healing.

As they concluded their discussion, the moon hung high in the sky, casting a serene light over the town. The group left the living room, their thoughts focused on the complex path that lay ahead. The understanding of the legal chessboard served as a reminder of the importance of balancing justice, accountability, and the human emotions that had led to this tragic chapter in Willowbrook's history.

Willowbrook's streets were no longer shrouded in mystery and fear. The town had faced its demons, uncovered the truth, and was now moving toward a place of healing. The group had navigated through layers of deception, motives, and emotions, and now, as they gathered once again in the living room of the Victorian house, their focus shifted to the crucial task of building a strong case that would connect the evidence to the culprit, ensuring that justice would be served.

Detective Thompson's voice was determined as she addressed the group. "Our journey has led us here, to the point where we must connect the dots and build a case that leaves no room for doubt. The evidence we've gathered must lead us to the truth and hold the culprit accountable."

Amy nodded, her expression focused. "By meticulously connecting each piece of evidence to the culprit's actions and motivations, we can present a compelling case that stands up to scrutiny."

Mark leaned forward, his voice unwavering. "Let's approach this step with precision. Our commitment to justice demands that we leave no stone unturned."

As they reviewed the evidence they had collected – the cryptic notes, the symbols, the confrontations, and the emotional triggers – they began to weave together the narrative that would connect the evidence to the culprit's actions.

"The evidence should tell a story," Sarah observed. "A story that highlights the sequence of events and motivations that led to Evan's disappearance."

Daniel's voice was analytical. "We must consider every detail, every interaction, and every piece of information we've gathered. The case should be a cohesive puzzle that leaves no room for ambiguity."

With their insights in mind, they set out to construct the case – a case that would lay bare the sequence of events, the motivations, and the connections between the evidence and the culprit's actions.

"The cryptic notes were a tool of manipulation," Detective Thompson noted. "They were used to control events and divert attention away from the true motivations."

Amy added, "The symbols, the interactions with the suspects, and the conversations we had with the culprit – all of these elements must be woven together to create a comprehensive narrative."

Mark's expression was resolute. "We're not only presenting evidence, but also telling a story of how desperation, revenge, and broken bonds converged to create a tragic outcome."

As they discussed the building of the case, they realized that their efforts were a testament to their commitment to truth, justice, and the town's healing.

Sarah's voice was filled with determination. "The case we build is a reflection of our dedication to ensuring that the truth prevails and that justice is served."

Daniel added, "Through the meticulous connection of evidence, we can bring clarity to a story that was once shrouded in darkness."

The conversation was an exercise in precision and determination. The group's commitment to building a strong case that would connect the evidence to the culprit's actions was a testament to their unwavering pursuit of justice.

As they concluded their discussion, the room was filled with a sense of purpose. The moon's gentle light streamed through the windows, casting a calming glow over the town. The group left the living room, their thoughts focused on the task at hand. The understanding of building the case served as a reminder of the importance of diligence, meticulousness, and the pursuit of truth in ensuring that justice would be served for Evan and the town of Willowbrook.

The days turned into weeks, and Willowbrook found itself on the threshold of a pivotal moment – the trial that would determine the fate of the culprit and bring closure to the town's painful chapter. As the group gathered in the living room of the Victorian house, the weight of the impending courtroom drama hung heavy in the air. The evidence had been connected, the case had been built, and now, the trial of the birthday boy's murderer was about to unfold.

Detective Thompson's voice was composed as she addressed the group. "Our journey has led us here, to the threshold of justice. The trial will test our resolve and determination to ensure that the truth prevails."

Amy nodded, her expression resolute. "By presenting the evidence we've gathered and telling the story of what transpired, we can ensure that the town finds closure and healing."

Mark leaned forward, his voice steady. "Let's approach the trial with unwavering commitment. The courtroom drama is a culmination of our efforts to bring justice to Evan and the town of Willowbrook."

As they reviewed their strategy for the trial – the witnesses, the evidence, and the narrative they would present – they began to prepare for the drama that would unfold in the courtroom.

"The trial is a chance to connect the dots for the jury," Sarah observed. "We must guide them through the sequence of events and the motivations that led to this tragedy."

Daniel's voice was focused. "We need to anticipate challenges from the defense and be prepared to counter their arguments with the strength of our evidence."

With their insights in mind, they set out to finalize their trial strategy – a strategy that would ensure the evidence was presented in a way that left no room for doubt, that told a compelling story, and that honored the memory of Evan.
"The cryptic notes and symbols were tools of manipulation," Detective Thompson noted. "We need to reveal the true intentions behind them and the role they played in diverting attention from the culprit."
Amy added, "The emotional triggers, the broken bonds, and the motivations – all of these elements must be woven together to create a comprehensive narrative that explains the events that transpired."
Mark's expression was resolute. "Our commitment to justice should guide every aspect of our presentation. This trial is about seeking the truth and ensuring accountability."
As they discussed their trial strategy, they realized that their efforts were a reflection of their dedication to bringing justice to Evan and the town he had left behind.
Sarah's voice was filled with determination. "The courtroom drama is a culmination of the town's journey – a journey through darkness and deception to the pursuit of truth and healing."
Daniel added, "Our presentation should be a beacon of clarity in the midst of confusion, shedding light on the motivations and consequences of the actions that led to this tragedy."
The conversation was a combination of strategy, determination, and a sense of duty. The group's commitment to the courtroom drama was a testament to their dedication to ensuring that justice was served, not just for the town, but for the memory of Evan.
As they concluded their discussion, the moon's glow illuminated the room, casting a serene light over their preparations. The group left the living room, their thoughts focused on the courtroom drama that lay ahead. The understanding of the importance of presenting a strong case

in the trial served as a reminder of the significance of the pursuit of justice and closure in the town of Willowbrook.

LINGERING SHADOWS

The trial had come and gone, leaving Willowbrook with a sense of closure and justice. The town had faced its demons, unraveled the truth, and held the culprit accountable for their actions. As the group gathered in the living room of the Victorian house, the weight of the aftermath settled in – the emotional aftermath that accompanies the closure of a painful chapter. They turned their attention to the complex emotions that had emerged in the wake of the trial – the grief of loss and the burden of guilt that lingered in the hearts of those who had been touched by the tragedy.

Detective Thompson's voice was gentle as she addressed the group. "The trial was a step toward closure, but the aftermath of a tragedy is a complex journey of emotions. We must help the town navigate through grief and guilt."

Amy nodded, her expression compassionate. "By acknowledging these emotions and providing support, we can help the community heal and move forward."

Mark leaned forward, his voice filled with empathy. "Let's approach this phase with sensitivity. The aftermath is a time for healing, reflection, and rebuilding."

As they reviewed the impact of the trial – the emotions it had stirred, the wounds it had uncovered, and the relief it had brought – they began to discuss how to guide the town through the process of healing.

"Grief is a natural response to loss," Sarah observed. "But it can manifest differently in each individual. Our role is to create a supportive environment for people to express their feelings."

Daniel's voice was thoughtful. "Guilt can also be a powerful emotion, especially for those who feel they could have done more to prevent the tragedy. It's important to address this emotion with empathy and understanding."

With their insights in mind, they set out to provide support for the town's residents – to offer a safe space for grief and guilt, and to guide them through the process of healing.

"The trial might have brought closure, but the journey is far from over," Detective Thompson noted. "Our commitment to the town extends beyond the courtroom."

Amy added, "Healing is not linear. It's important to remember that people will progress at their own pace and in their own way."

Mark's expression was reassuring. "Our presence and support can help the town as it navigates through the complexities of grief and guilt."

As they discussed the aftermath of the tragedy, they realized that their efforts were a reflection of their commitment to the well-being of the town and its residents.

Sarah's voice was filled with compassion. "The aftermath is a time for the town to come together, to support one another, and to find strength in shared experiences."

Daniel added, "Through understanding, empathy, and community, we can guide the town toward healing and a brighter future."

The conversation was an affirmation of their dedication to the well-being of the town. The group's commitment to navigating through the aftermath of the tragedy was a testament to their understanding of the emotional complexities that come with closure and healing.

As they concluded their discussion, the room was enveloped ˋ sense of unity. The moon's soft light illuminated the room, ˋ peaceful atmosphere over the space. The group left the living room, their thoughts focused on the journey that lay ahead. The understanding of the aftermath of a tragedy served as a reminder of the importance of empathy, support, and community in the process of healing and moving forward in Willowbrook.

In the wake of the trial and the subsequent aftermath, Willowbrook found itself at a crossroads – a juncture where the town could begin the process of healing and rebuilding. The group had navigated through deception, motivations, and emotions, and now, as they gathered in the living room of the Victorian house, their focus shifted to the important task of healing the wounds that had been left behind by the loss of Evan and the tragedy that had gripped the town.

Detective Thompson's voice was tender as she addressed the group. "Healing is a vital step as the town moves forward. We must guide the community toward a path of recovery and rebuilding."

Amy nodded, her expression hopeful. "By fostering an environment of support, understanding, and renewal, we can help the town mend its wounds and emerge stronger."

Mark leaned forward, his voice filled with compassion. "Let's approach this phase with patience and dedication. The healing process is a journey, and we must be there to provide guidance and solace."

As they reviewed the impact of the trial and the emotions that had been stirred, they began to discuss the ways in which the town could move toward healing and rebuild lives that had been affected by the loss.

"Healing is not a linear process," Sarah observed. "It involves acknowledging pain, finding healthy outlets for emotions, and seeking connection within the community."

Daniel's voice was reflective. "The town's strength lies in its ability to come together, support one another, and find a sense of purpose beyond the tragedy."

With their insights in mind, they set out to guide the town through the healing process – a process that would require patience, empathy, and a shared commitment to moving forward.

"The trial and the aftermath have taken a toll," Detective Thompson noted. "But they have also illuminated the town's resilience and capacity for renewal."

Amy added, "It's important to provide resources for counseling, support groups, and outlets for creative expression. These can aid the healing process and offer individuals ways to process their emotions."

Mark's expression was hopeful. "As we guide the town toward healing, we also have an opportunity to focus on positive change and growth."

As they discussed the healing process, they realized that their efforts were a testament to their commitment to the well-being of the town's residents.

Sarah's voice was filled with hope. "Healing is a journey that can lead to renewed connections, a deeper understanding of one another, and a stronger sense of community."

Daniel added, "Through compassion, understanding, and resilience, we can help the town transform its wounds into sources of strength."

The conversation was an affirmation of their dedication to the town's recovery. The group's commitment to healing the wounds left behind by loss was a testament to their understanding of the importance of renewal, support, and the power of community in the face of adversity.

As they concluded their discussion, the room was suffused with a sense of purpose. The moon's glow filtered through the windows, casting a serene light over the space. The group left the living room, their thoughts focused on the journey of healing that lay ahead. The understanding of healing the ˙ınds served as a reminder of the importance of compassion, perseverance, and community in the process of rebuilding lives and finding strength in Willowbrook.

Time had passed, and Willowbrook had taken its first steps toward healing. The town had faced deception, unravelled motivations, and navigated through the tumultuous aftermath. As the group gathered in the living room of the Victorian house, a subtle undercurrent of unease lingered beneath the surface – a reminder of the legacy of death that the tragedy had left behind. They turned their attention to the complex emotions that arise when a community is confronted with the lingering ghost of a celebration that had turned into a nightmare.

Detective Thompson's voice was somber as she addressed the group. "The legacy of a tragedy can cast a long shadow, affecting how a community views celebrations and milestones. We must address these emotions as the town seeks to rebuild."

Amy nodded, her expression contemplative. "By acknowledging the complexities of the legacy and offering a space for reflection, we can help the town find a way to honor the past while embracing the future."

Mark leaned forward, his voice filled with understanding. "Let's approach this phase with empathy. Confronting the ghost of celebration is an essential step in the healing journey."

As they reviewed the impact of the trial and the healing process, they began to discuss the emotions that surrounded the idea of celebrating in a town that had been touched by tragedy.

"The legacy of death can cast a pall over celebrations," Sarah observed. "People may feel conflicted about finding joy in the midst of a painful history."

Daniel's voice was reflective. "Confronting the ghost of celebration is an opportunity for the town to redefine its relationship with events that mark milestones and happiness."

With their insights in mind, they set out to guide the town through the process of confronting the legacy of death – a process that required sensitivity, introspection, and a shared commitment to finding a balance between honoring the past and embracing the future.

"The town's identity has been forever altered by the tragedy," Detective Thompson noted. "But it's possible to find a way to celebrate while still acknowledging the pain."

Amy added, "Creating new traditions and rituals that honor the memory of those lost can provide a sense of closure and a way to move forward."

Mark's expression was empathetic. "We must remember that confronting the legacy is a journey of both individual and collective healing."

As they discussed the legacy of death and celebration, they realized that their efforts were a reflection of their commitment to helping the town find a way to reconcile the past with the present.

Sarah's voice was filled with hope. "Confronting the legacy is a way for the town to reclaim its sense of identity and resilience."

Daniel added, "Through reflection, empathy, and unity, we can help the town navigate the complex emotions that arise when celebrating in the wake of tragedy."

The conversation was an affirmation of their dedication to the town's well-being. The group's commitment to confronting the legacy of death and celebration was a testament to their understanding of the importance of finding a path that honors the past, supports healing, and embraces the future.

As they concluded their discussion, a sense of unity pervaded the room. The moon's gentle light illuminated the space, casting a tranquil atmosphere over the scene. The group left the living room, their thoughts focused on the journey of ⁻onting the legacy that lay ahead. The understanding of ⸱ of celebration served as a reminder of the importance of sensitivity, reflection, and community in the process of navigating the complexities of emotion in Willowbrook.

RESIDUAL FEARS

Willowbrook had embarked on a journey of healing, confronting the truth, and rebuilding in the aftermath of the tragedy. However, as time passed, a palpable sense of lingering paranoia had settled within the community. The group had faced deception, motivations, and emotions, yet the town still struggled to shake off the shadows of the past. As they gathered in the living room of the Victorian house, they turned their attention to the complex emotions that accompanied the community's struggle to move on while grappling with lingering paranoia.

Detective Thompson's voice was empathetic as she addressed the group. "Moving on after a tragedy is a challenging process, often accompanied by lingering fears and doubts. We must help the town navigate through this phase with patience and understanding."

Amy nodded, her expression thoughtful. "By acknowledging the emotions of lingering paranoia and providing reassurance, we can guide the community toward a place of greater security and peace."

Mark leaned forward, his voice filled with compassion. "Let's approach this phase with empathy. Lingering paranoia is a natural response to trauma, and we must be there to provide support."

As they reviewed the progress the town had made, they began to discuss the emotions that surfaced when a community struggled to move on while contending with lingering paranoia.

"The tragedy has left a lasting impact on people's sense of safety," Sarah observed. "Lingering paranoia can lead to heightened vigilance and fear of potential threats."

Daniel's voice was reflective. "As the community grapples with moving on, it's important to address the fears and uncertainties that linger beneath the surface."

With their insights in mind, they set out to guide the town through the process of facing lingering paranoia – a process that required patience, reassurance, and a shared commitment to rebuilding a sense of security.

"The legacy of fear can be a difficult burden to bear," Detective Thompson noted. "But by providing resources for counseling and support, we can help the town address these feelings."

Amy added, "Community engagement and open conversations can provide reassurance and remind people that they are not alone in their fears."

Mark's expression was supportive. "As we guide the town toward healing, we must also help them confront and gradually overcome their lingering paranoia."

As they discussed the struggles of moving on while dealing with lingering paranoia, they realized that their efforts were a testament to their commitment to the town's overall well-being.

Sarah's voice was filled with hope. "Lingering paranoia is a phase that the town can navigate through with time, support, and a collective effort to rebuild a sense of safety."

Daniel added, "Through empathy, understanding, and community solidarity, we can help the town find a way to move beyond the shadows of the past."

The conversation was a reminder of their dedication to the town's continued healing. The group's commitment to guiding the community through the struggles of moving on while facing lingering paranoia was a testament to their understanding of the importance of empathy, reassurance, and unity in the process of overcoming trauma in Willowbrook.

As they concluded their discussion, a sense of determination filled the room. The moon's soft light illuminated the space, casting a gentle atmosphere over their deliberations. The group left the living room, their thoughts focused on the journey of addressing lingering paranoia that lay ahead. The understanding of this phase served as a reminder of the importance of patience, reassurance, and a shared commitment to healing in the town of Willowbrook.

As the town of Willowbrook slowly but surely moved forward in its journey of healing, a new challenge emerged – haunting memories that refused to fade. The group had confronted deception, motivations, and the aftermath of the tragedy, yet the incident continued to cast its shadow through the haunting nightmares and distressing flashbacks that plagued the community. Gathered once more in the living room of the Victorian house, they turned their attention to the complex emotions that arose when memories of the incident refused to let go.

Detective Thompson's voice was compassionate as she addressed the group. "Healing is not always linear, and haunting memories can be a painful reminder of the trauma that the community has endured. We must help the town navigate through this phase with empathy and support."

Amy nodded, her expression reflective. "By acknowledging the distressing memories and providing tools to manage them, we can guide the community toward a place of healing and resilience."

Mark leaned forward, his voice filled with understanding. "Let's approach this phase with patience and sensitivity. Haunting memories are a normal response to trauma, and we must be there to offer solace."

As they reviewed the progress the town had made, they began to discuss the emotions that accompanied the persistent nightmares and flashbacks of the incident.

"The mind often replays traumatic events as a way of processing," Sarah observed. "But this can lead to distressing flashbacks and nightmares that disrupt daily life."

Daniel's voice was thoughtful. "As the community seeks to heal, it's crucial to provide resources for managing these memories and finding a sense of control."

With their insights in mind, they set out to guide the town through the process of addressing haunting memories – a process that required understanding, self-care, and a shared commitment to finding ways to manage the distress.

"The nightmares and flashbacks are a reminder of the trauma's impact," Detective Thompson noted. "But with the right tools, the community can learn to cope and find a path toward healing."

Amy added, "Education on managing triggers, mindfulness techniques, and seeking professional help can provide individuals with the tools they need to navigate through distressing memories."

Mark's expression was reassuring. "As we guide the town toward healing, we must also help them develop strategies to overcome the haunting memories that persist."

As they discussed the challenges of addressing haunting memories, they realized that their efforts were a testament to their commitment to the town's continued well-being.

Sarah's voice was filled with hope. "Haunting memories can be managed, and the community can find a way to regain a sense of control over their thoughts and emotions."

Daniel added, "Through empathy, support, and resilience, we can help the town learn to manage the memories that linger and find a path toward emotional recovery."

The conversation was a reaffirmation of their dedication to the town's healing journey. The group's commitment to guiding the community through the challenges of addressing haunting memories was a testament to their understanding of the importance of empathy, education, and shared strength in the process of overcoming trauma in Willowbrook.

As they concluded their discussion, a sense of unity filled the room. The moon's serene light illuminated the space, casting a gentle atmosphere over their deliberations. The group left the living room, their thoughts focused on the journey of addressing haunting memories that lay ahead. The understanding of this phase served as a reminder of the importance of support, resilience, and the power of community in the process of healing and recovery in Willowbrook.

As Willowbrook continued on its path of healing, a sense of cautiousness lingered beneath the surface. The town had confronted deception, motivations, and the aftermath of the tragedy, yet the specter of danger still loomed, casting doubt over celebrations and gatherings. Gathered once more in the living room of the Victorian house, the group turned their attention to the complex emotions that accompanied the perceived danger amidst the community's attempts to reclaim normalcy and joy.

Detective Thompson's voice was empathetic as she addressed the group. "The process of healing is an intricate one, and perceived danger can create fractures in the town's attempts to move forward. We must guide the community with understanding and support."

Amy nodded, her expression contemplative. "By acknowledging the fears and offering reassurance, we can help the community find a way to celebrate without letting doubt overshadow their efforts."

Mark leaned forward, his voice filled with empathy. "Let's approach this phase with patience and sensitivity. The perceived danger is a reminder of the town's vulnerability, and we must be there to provide comfort."

As they reviewed the progress the town had made, they began to discuss the emotions that accompanied the unease that arose when celebrations were tinged with a sense of perceived danger.

"Trauma can leave a mark on how people perceive safety," Sarah observed. "Perceived danger can lead to heightened vigilance and fear of potential threats, even in celebratory settings."

Daniel's voice was reflective. "As the community strives to find joy and normalcy, it's essential to address the fears and uncertainties that cast shadows on their efforts."

With their insights in mind, they set out to guide the town through the process of navigating perceived danger – a process that required understanding, reassurance, and a shared commitment to creating an environment of safety.

"The perceived danger is a reflection of the town's vulnerability," Detective Thompson noted. "But by providing information on safety measures and creating open dialogues, we can help the community rebuild their sense of security."

Amy added, "Education on recognizing triggers, fostering community connections, and seeking support can help individuals manage their fears and anxieties."

Mark's expression was supportive. "As we guide the town toward healing, we must also help them reclaim their sense of safety while celebrating life's moments."

As they discussed the challenges of addressing perceived danger, they realized that their efforts were a testament to their commitment to the town's overall well-being.

Sarah's voice was filled with hope. "Perceived danger is a phase that the town can overcome with time, information, and collective effort to rebuild their sense of security."

Daniel added, "Through empathy, communication, and community solidarity, we can help the town navigate through the complexities of perceived danger and reclaim their ability to celebrate."

The conversation was a reminder of their dedication to the town's continued healing. The group's commitment to guiding the community through the challenges of perceived danger was a testament to their understanding of the importance of empathy, reassurance, and unity in the process of overcoming trauma in Willowbrook.

As they concluded their discussion, a sense of determination filled the room. The moon's soft light illuminated the space, casting a gentle atmosphere over their deliberations. The group left the living room, their thoughts focused on the journey of addressing perceived danger that lay ahead. The understanding of this phase served as a reminder of the importance of patience, reassurance, and a shared commitment to healing in the town of Willowbrook.

CLOSURE AND REFLECTION

The town of Willowbrook had come a long way on its journey of healing. It had faced deception, motivations, and the complex aftermath of a tragedy that had gripped the community. As they gathered in the living room of the Victorian house, a sense of progress and closure filled the air. The group turned their attention to the profound role that justice had played in the healing process – the process of finding closure and a sense of resolution that had allowed the community to move forward.

Detective Thompson's voice was reflective as she addressed the group. "Justice has been a guiding force on this journey. It's not just about accountability for the perpetrator; it's about providing closure and a sense of validation for the community."

Amy nodded, her expression filled with understanding. "By ensuring that justice was served, we've helped the town find a way to heal and move beyond the darkness that once engulfed it."

Mark leaned forward, his voice resolute. "Let's remember that justice is a beacon of hope. It's a reminder that the truth prevails and that healing is possible even in the face of adversity."

As they reviewed the progress the town had made, they began to discuss the profound impact that the pursuit of justice had on the healing process.

"Justice is more than just legal proceedings," Sarah observed. "It's a process that validates the experiences of the community and empowers them to reclaim their sense of security."

Daniel's voice was thoughtful. "As the community seeks closure, the pursuit of justice acts as a bridge that connects the past to a future of healing and renewal."

With their insights in mind, they set out to reflect on the role justice had played in the town's healing journey – a role that had gone beyond legal proceedings to become a fundamental aspect of the town's collective recovery.

"The trial and the pursuit of justice were about honoring Evan's memory and seeking truth," Detective Thompson noted. "But they were also about providing the community with closure and a sense of justice served."

Amy added, "Through justice, we've helped the town find a way to come to terms with the tragedy and move beyond the pain that once held them captive."

Mark's expression was filled with hope. "Justice is a testament to the town's strength and resilience. It's a reminder that even in the face of darkness, light can shine through."

As they discussed the profound impact of justice, they realized that their efforts were a testament to their commitment to the well-being of the town.

Sarah's voice was filled with conviction. "The healing process, guided by justice, has been a journey of transformation – from despair to hope, from chaos to understanding."

Daniel added, "Through dedication, empathy, and unwavering commitment to truth, justice has played a crucial role in helping the town find closure and healing."

The conversation was a reaffirmation of their dedication to the town's recovery. The group's commitment to the healing process, guided by justice, was a testament to their understanding of the importance of accountability, closure, and the power of community in the face of adversity.

As they concluded their discussion, a sense of unity pervaded the room. The moon's serene light filtered through the windows, casting a peaceful atmosphere over the scene. The group left the living room, their thoughts focused on the continued journey of healing that lay ahead. The understanding of the healing process through justice served as a reminder of the importance of truth, closure, and community in the process of finding healing and renewal in Willowbrook.

As time passed and Willowbrook continued its journey of healing, the memory of Evan, the birthday boy who had tragically lost his life, remained a guiding light for the community. Gathered in the living room of the Victorian house, the group turned their attention to the profound importance of remembering Evan – not just for the tragedy he was a part of, but for the life he had lived and the legacy he had left behind.

Detective Thompson's voice was heartfelt as she addressed the group. "Evan's memory is a testament to the resilience of the human spirit. As we honor his life, we're also reminding ourselves of the importance of cherishing every moment."

Amy nodded, her expression filled with warmth. "By remembering Evan's passions, his dreams, and the joy he brought to others, we can inspire the community to live fully and embrace life."

Mark leaned forward, his voice gentle. "Let's approach this phase with reverence and gratitude. Remembering Evan is not just about the past; it's about the legacy that lives on through our actions."

As they reviewed the progress the town had made, they began to discuss the ways in which they could honor Evan's memory and celebrate the life he had lived.

"Evan's memory is intertwined with the town's journey," Sarah observed. "It's a reminder that even in the face of tragedy, his spirit lives on through the strength and resilience of the community."

Daniel's voice was reflective. "As the community moves forward, it's essential to incorporate Evan's memory into the fabric of its identity – a reminder of the importance of cherishing every day."

With their insights in mind, they set out to guide the town through the process of remembering Evan – a process that required reverence, celebration, and a shared commitment to living life to the fullest.

"Evan's memory is a source of inspiration," Detective Thompson noted. "Through events, memorials, and community initiatives, we can honor his legacy and remind ourselves of the fragility and preciousness of life."

Amy added, "Remembering Evan is a way to weave his spirit into the town's ongoing journey of healing, growth, and resilience."

Mark's expression was filled with gratitude. "As we remember Evan, we're also acknowledging the importance of embracing life's opportunities and spreading the light of positivity."

As they discussed the ways to honor Evan's memory, they realized that their efforts were a testament to their commitment to the town's ongoing well-being.

Sarah's voice was filled with appreciation. "Remembering Evan is a celebration of life itself – a reminder that his legacy continues to inspire and uplift the community."

Daniel added, "Through remembrance, dedication, and the shared commitment to cherish each day, we can ensure that Evan's spirit lives on in the heart of Willowbrook."

The conversation was a celebration of Evan's life and a reaffirmation of their dedication to the town's ongoing recovery. The group's commitment to remembering the birthday boy was a testament to their understanding of the importance of inspiration, gratitude, and community in the process of finding healing and renewal in Willowbrook.

As they concluded their discussion, a sense of unity filled the room. The moon's gentle light illuminated the space, casting a peaceful atmosphere over their deliberations. The group left the living room, their thoughts focused on the journey of remembering Evan and the legacy of positivity and inspiration that he had left behind. The understanding of this phase served as a reminder of the importance of cherishing life, celebrating memories, and fostering a sense of community in the town of Willowbrook.

As Willowbrook continued to heal and rebuild, the impact of the tragedy had left profound lessons etched in the hearts of the community. Gathered in the living room of the Victorian house, the group turned their attention to the lasting impact on relationships and celebrations – the realization that every connection and moment of joy was precious and should never be taken for granted.

Detective Thompson's voice was contemplative as she addressed the group. "Tragedy has a way of reshaping our perspective on life. It teaches us to value relationships and celebrations, as they become reminders of the preciousness of every moment."

Amy nodded, her expression filled with empathy. "By acknowledging the lessons we've learned, we can guide the community to forge deeper connections and celebrate with a renewed sense of gratitude."

Mark leaned forward, his voice filled with introspection. "Let's approach this phase with humility and mindfulness. The lessons from tragedy are a constant reminder to cherish our loved ones and find joy in every occasion."

As they reviewed the progress the town had made, they began to discuss the ways in which the lessons from the tragedy had impacted relationships and celebrations.

"Tragedy can strengthen bonds as people come together for support," Sarah observed. "It's a reminder that relationships are the foundation that sustains us through difficult times."

Daniel's voice was reflective. "As the community seeks to rebuild, the lessons learned serve as a guiding compass, shaping the way they navigate connections and moments of joy."

With their insights in mind, they set out to guide the town through the process of embracing the lessons learned from the tragedy – a process that required vulnerability, gratitude, and a shared commitment to fostering meaningful connections.

"The tragedy has illuminated the importance of empathy and communication," Detective Thompson noted. "Through open dialogues and acts of kindness, we can help the community build stronger, more resilient relationships."

Amy added, "Lessons from tragedy are a reminder to celebrate with intention – to cherish every gathering, every moment of laughter, and every milestone."

Mark's expression was filled with wisdom. "As we navigate through relationships and celebrations, let's carry the lessons with us, allowing them to shape the way we interact with others and embrace happiness."

As they discussed the impact on relationships and celebrations, they realized that their efforts were a testament to their commitment to the town's ongoing well-being.

Sarah's voice was filled with hope. "The lessons from tragedy are a beacon of light that guide us toward deeper connections and a greater appreciation for life's joys."

Daniel added, "Through remembrance, dedication, and the shared commitment to the lessons learned, we can honor the past and build a stronger, more compassionate community."

The conversation was a celebration of growth and a reaffirmation of their dedication to the town's ongoing recovery. The group's commitment to embracing the lessons from tragedy was a testament to their understanding of the importance of empathy, gratitude, and community in the process of finding healing and renewal in Willowbrook.

As they concluded their discussion, a sense of unity pervaded the room. The moon's serene light filtered through the windows, casting a tranquil atmosphere over the scene. The group left the living room, their thoughts focused on the journey of embracing the lessons from tragedy that lay ahead. The understanding of this phase served as a reminder of the importance of cherishing relationships, finding joy in celebrations, and fostering a sense of community in the town of Willowbrook.

THE UNFORGOTTEN MYSTERY

As Willowbrook continued its journey of healing, there were certain shadows that seemed reluctant to fade. The town had confronted deception, motivations, and the aftermath of a tragedy, yet lingering questions and unsolved puzzles still cast doubt over the community. Gathered in the living room of the Victorian house, the group turned their attention to the complex emotions that accompanied the presence of shadows of doubt – the unanswered mysteries that refused to be forgotten.

Detective Thompson's voice was contemplative as she addressed the group. "The journey toward healing is often accompanied by questions that linger. These shadows of doubt remind us that some puzzles may never be fully solved."

Amy nodded, her expression filled with empathy. "By acknowledging these uncertainties and offering solace, we can help the community find a way to navigate the space between what is known and what remains a mystery."

Mark leaned forward, his voice filled with understanding. "Let's approach this phase with patience and openness. The shadows of doubt are a reminder that life is complex, and some answers may forever elude us."

As they reviewed the progress the town had made, they began to discuss the emotions that accompanied the presence of unanswered questions and lingering mysteries.

"The mind seeks closure," Sarah observed. "Unsolved puzzles can lead to a sense of unease and a longing for answers that may never come."

Daniel's voice was reflective. "As the community seeks to move forward, it's essential to address the uncertainty and create a space for acceptance of the unknown."

With their insights in mind, they set out to guide the town through the process of facing the shadows of doubt – a process that required understanding, acceptance, and a shared commitment to finding solace in the midst of uncertainty.

"The shadows of doubt are a reminder of the limits of human understanding," Detective Thompson noted. "By providing support and encouraging dialogue, we can help the community find a way to find peace even in the face of unanswered questions."

Amy added, "Education on managing uncertainties, seeking closure through other means, and finding strength in the community can help individuals cope with the lingering mysteries."

Mark's expression was reassuring. "As we guide the town toward healing, we must also help them find ways to come to terms with the shadows of doubt that may always be a part of their story."

As they discussed the challenges of addressing shadows of doubt, they realized that their efforts were a testament to their commitment to the town's ongoing well-being.

Sarah's voice was filled with hope. "Navigating uncertainties is a phase that the community can manage with time, support, and a shared commitment to finding solace in their resilience."

Daniel added, "Through empathy, understanding, and unity, we can help the town learn to coexist with the shadows of doubt and find a path toward emotional recovery."

The conversation was a reminder of their dedication to the town's continued healing. The group's commitment to guiding the community through the challenges of facing lingering mysteries was a testament to their understanding of the importance of empathy, acceptance, and shared strength in the process of overcoming trauma in Willowbrook.

As they concluded their discussion, a sense of unity filled the room. The moon's gentle light illuminated the space, casting a tranquil atmosphere over their deliberations. The group left the living room, their thoughts focused on the journey of facing shadows of doubt that lay ahead. The understanding of this phase served as a reminder of the importance of support, resilience, and the power of community in the process of healing and recovery in Willowbrook.

In the wake of tragedy, some mysteries have a way of persisting, defying time and reason. Willowbrook had confronted deception, motivations, and the intricate aftermath of a tragedy, yet certain hidden truths continued to evade discovery. Gathered in the living room of the Victorian house, the group turned their attention to the tenacious pursuit of truth – the unending investigations that kept the community's curiosity alive.

Detective Thompson's voice was determined as she addressed the group. "The quest for truth is unwavering. Some mysteries may elude us, but the pursuit of hidden truths is a testament to our commitment to justice and understanding."

Amy nodded, her expression resolute. "By acknowledging the persistent questions and keeping the search alive, we can guide the community to continue seeking answers, even in the face of uncertainty."

Mark leaned forward, his voice filled with resolve. "Let's approach this phase with determination and integrity. The eternal investigations remind us that truth is worth pursuing, no matter how elusive it may seem."

As they reviewed the progress the town had made, they began to discuss the emotions that accompanied the unending quest for uncovering hidden truths.

"Curiosity is a driving force," Sarah observed. "Eternal investigations can lead to a sense of purpose and a commitment to honoring the memory of those affected by the tragedy."

Daniel's voice was reflective. "As the community seeks understanding, it's essential to embrace the journey of discovery, even if it takes us down unexpected paths."

With their insights in mind, they set out to guide the town through the process of continuing the pursuit of hidden truths – a process that required determination, patience, and a shared commitment to seeking answers.

"The eternal investigations are a reminder of our dedication to the truth," Detective Thompson noted. "By providing resources for research, promoting open dialogue, and encouraging collaboration, we can help the community find ways to continue their quest for understanding."

Amy added, "Education on investigative techniques, cultivating a sense of unity, and promoting the importance of preserving history can help individuals remain engaged in the pursuit of hidden truths."

Mark's expression was unwavering. "As we guide the town toward healing, we must also support them in maintaining their commitment to uncovering hidden truths, even as time moves forward."

As they discussed the challenges of continuing the quest for hidden truths, they realized that their efforts were a testament to their commitment to the town's ongoing well-being.

Sarah's voice was filled with hope. "Eternal investigations are a testament to the community's resilience and their unwavering dedication to honoring the past and seeking justice."

Daniel added, "Through empathy, curiosity, and shared determination, we can help the town navigate the complexities of uncovering hidden truths and find a sense of purpose in the process."

The conversation was a celebration of perseverance and a reaffirmation of their dedication to the town's ongoing recovery. The group's commitment to the eternal investigations was a testament to their understanding of the importance of truth, justice, and community in the process of finding healing and renewal in Willowbrook.

As they concluded their discussion, a sense of unity pervaded the room. The moon's serene light filtered through the windows, casting a peaceful atmosphere over the scene. The group left the living room, their thoughts focused on the journey of continuing the quest for hidden truths that lay ahead. The understanding of this phase served as a reminder of the importance of determination, integrity, and the power of community in the town of Willowbrook.

In the aftermath of tragedy, certain stories have a way of transcending time, becoming enigmas that continue to intrigue and captivate. Willowbrook had faced deception, motivations, and the intricate aftermath of a tragedy that had forever altered the community. Yet, amid the healing, there was an echo of enigma that remained, a tale that was never fully laid to rest. Gathered in the living room of the Victorian house, the group turned their attention to the lasting impact of these mysterious echoes – the stories that defied closure and continued to leave their mark.

Detective Thompson's voice was contemplative as she addressed the group. "Enigmas have a way of lingering, reminding us that some stories are never fully told. They leave an imprint, encouraging us to seek the deeper layers of truth."

Amy nodded, her expression thoughtful. "By acknowledging the allure of these echoes and delving into their mysteries, we can guide the community to embrace the complexity of life's narratives."

Mark leaned forward, his voice filled with curiosity. "Let's approach this phase with a sense of wonder and exploration.

The echoes of enigma invite us to uncover hidden layers and appreciate the mysteries that make life intriguing."

As they reviewed the progress the town had made, they began to discuss the emotions that accompanied the echoes of enigma – the tales that continued to weave their threads in the fabric of the community's collective memory.

"Some stories are destined to remain unfinished," Sarah observed. "Echoes of enigma can evoke a sense of curiosity, prompting us to imagine the untold chapters."

Daniel's voice was reflective. "As the community moves forward, it's essential to embrace the allure of these echoes, recognizing that they enrich the tapestry of our experiences."

With their insights in mind, they set out to guide the town through the process of embracing the echoes of enigma – a process that required curiosity, acceptance, and a shared commitment to exploring the layers of untold stories.

"The echoes of enigma are reminders of the complexity of human existence," Detective Thompson noted. "By providing opportunities for storytelling, creative expression, and the sharing of diverse perspectives, we can help the community find ways to engage with these enigmas."

Amy added, "Education on the power of narratives, fostering an environment of open-mindedness, and encouraging exploration of unanswered questions can help individuals appreciate the beauty of life's mysteries."

Mark's expression was appreciative. "As we guide the town toward healing, we must also help them discover the value in embracing the echoes of enigma that enrich their journey."

As they discussed the challenges of embracing the echoes of enigma, they realized that their efforts were a testament to their commitment to the town's ongoing well-being.

Sarah's voice was filled with hope. "The echoes of enigma invite us to celebrate the beauty of unanswered questions and the wonder of life's enigmatic tales."

Daniel added, "Through curiosity, exploration, and a shared commitment to embracing mystery, we can help the town navigate the complexities of these lingering echoes and find a sense of fulfillment in their ongoing journey."

The conversation was a celebration of curiosity and a reaffirmation of their dedication to the town's ongoing recovery. The group's commitment to embracing the echoes of enigma was a testament to their understanding of the importance of embracing complexity, seeking wonder, and fostering a sense of community in the process of finding healing and renewal in Willowbrook.

As they concluded their discussion, a sense of unity pervaded the room. The moon's serene light filtered through the windows, casting a tranquil atmosphere over the scene. The group left the living room, their thoughts focused on the journey of embracing the echoes of enigma that lay ahead. The understanding of this phase served as a reminder of the importance of storytelling, wonder, and the power of community in the town of Willowbrook.

Printed in Great Britain
by Amazon

d025855a-7aba-439e-b320-598de956e82fR01